Marend of Marloven Hess

RELATED BOOKS IN THE SARTORIAS-DELES SEQUENCE

Senrid

Spy Princess

Sartor

Fleeing Peace

A Stranger to Command

The Rise of the Alliance Series

A Sword Named Truth

The Blood Mage Texts

The Hunters and the Hunted

Nightside of the Sun

The Norsunder War

Ship Without Sails

Marend of Marloven Hess

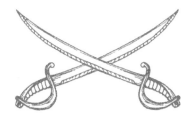

SHERWOOD SMITH

BOOK VIEW CAFE

BOOK VIEW CAFÉ

Published by Book View Café
304 S. Jones Blvd., Suite #2906
Las Vegas, NV 89107
www.bookviewcafe.com

ISBN: 978-1-63632-089-2

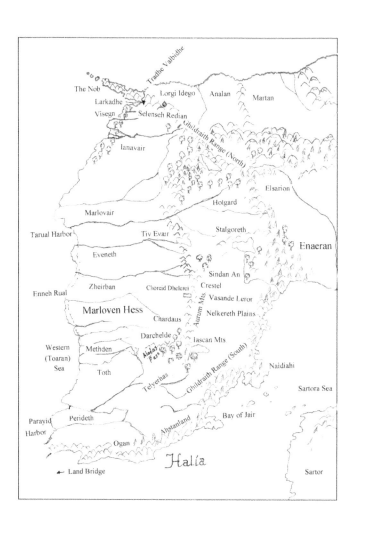

The Nob

Tradhe Valbidhe

Larkadhe

Lorgi Idego   Analan   Martan

Visegn   Selenseh Redian

Ghildraith Range (North)

Ianavair

Elsarion

Holgard

Marlovair

Stalgoreth

Tarual Harbor

Tiv Evair   Enaeran

Eveneth

Sindan An

Zheirban   Choreid Dhelerei   Crestel

Enneh Rual   Vasande Leror

Marloven Hess   Nelkereth Plains

Chardaus

Darchelde   Iascan Mts.

Western   Methden   Aldai
(Toaran)   Pass
Sea   Naidiahi

Toth   Ghildraith Range (South)

Aurum Mts.

Telyerhas   Sartora Sea

Parayid   Perideth   Bay of Jair
Harbor

Ahstanland

Ogan

Halia   Sartor

← Land Bridge

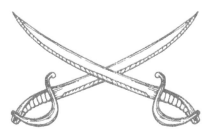

One

THIS IS HARDER TO write than I thought.

I think I had better start with losing Methden.

I'll begin when the academy seniors had all been sent home, and after them next year's seniors. They were wild with anger at being treated like babies. Especially after the triumphant battle at the river. But one battle is not the war—that's what everyone said to one another, sometimes with a little smile—because no one believed that Norsunder would beat us. Not on our own ground. Some of the older teens, including those never in the academy, ran to fight despite the orders to lie low, and didn't return.

Then my father, Jarl Jarend Ndarga of Methden, was killed. After that, every messenger's words brought another sword stroke to the heart.

The rest of us spent our days and nights running. We scavenged arrows. We begged farther and farther into the city for bandages, listerblossom, willow-steep, and the like, when the garrison healers ran out of supplies. The garrison became a lazarette of wounded, angry warriors determined to rise and get back to defend the kingdom.

That ended abruptly as a snuffed candle when word came that the new Harskiald, the hero Retren Forthan, had struck his banner at Aladas Pass.

You hear about striking the banner. It's in a lot of the saddest and most warlike ballads, the ones requiring at least five drums. Though it had been centuries since it had last happened, we all knew what it meant: that everyone, from the rankers to the runners, had died in a battle. And the commander, in this case the Harskiald, who had never lost a wargame, had slashed the banner himself so that it would not fall into Norsundrian hands, before turning his sword on himself.

That news stunned us as if a gigantic hand had slapped us all to the ground. And still more bad news came. Now the enemies were converging on the royal city.

There was another thing I'd heard *about*, but had never actually *heard*: all the old people singing the weird mourning ballad called the Andahi Lament. They sang it again and again, all through the night before the memorial for my father and the others of Methden who had fallen. They sang through the memorial, which was carried out under the eyes of the enemy, on a frigidly cold day, the sunlight mercilessly clear. Too many were Disappeared that day, my father, Jarend Ndarga, Jarl of Methden, the first.

For my brother Retren and me, resistance started that day.

Here is another beginning. I said this was hard. It was a Fifthday morning. Raining. Mother wept in her room. But everyone who knew she was weeping also knew she was a foreigner so Retren and I didn't get any shame. And Lesra was too young to care about appearing to be weak.

Retren didn't say anything and neither did I, but I knew he was missing Da, too. It was the day after the memorial. He and I met to plan revenge. What to do was obvious — kill Norsundrians — it was the number that had to be settled. I'd said one for each year of our lives but he scowled and said it was fine for *me* because I was fourteen, but he got cheated because he was not quite eleven. I reminded him that he could kill as many as he wanted, only they'd be for him not for Da, but I could see his point, so we decided in the end to do one for every year of Da's life, divided in half. (And if one did their half first, they'd keep their mouth shut till the other caught up.)

I set myself a goal: I had to kill mine within the same amount of time the Norsundrians had taken to invade. I thought, if I can kill that many in the same time, then they're not tougher than us. They just had cheats like magic, or something.

Easy to decide, but difficult to achieve.

There weren't too many Norsundrians in Methden, as most were attacking Choreid Dhelerei. I only got one the second night, and I wasn't sure he was dead. The following two days I couldn't find any lone ones to shoot without being seen doing it. I roamed the streets both days, and lurked around the garrison, which was next to empty, waiting. The Norsundrians who were there went about in groups, steel bare, and anyone, especially men, who even looked at them wrong got attacked and beaten. A couple were killed. Retren and I stayed away from the garrison until Commander Herid returned from the royal city, sent by the king.

I was sitting in the map room with young Sereth (or Sereth, I guess, since Old Sereth died of his wounds the second day) playing cards'n'shards. Commander Herid walked in, looking strange in the face. His uniform was gone. He wore carter's clothes, worn and dirty. Sereth and I both stood up (I always stuck to army protocol when I hung around the garrison, my choice, and they were used to it) and the garrison commander's eyes flicked over us as he slammed the door shut behind him.

"Lost the royal city?" I said.

He sat down heavily in his chair, looking so strange in civilian dress. "Yes. Lost, and heavy losses. Including the little princess."

"What?" That was several voices at once.

"And the king?" Sereth asked.

"Fought in the thick to the very end. In fact, four of them dragged him away when we decided to go to ground. There were just too many of them. Too many of us dying." He lowered his voice. "I was told he did the sword dance. All alone. Before the princess's bier."

Everyone looked away, or down, at that. I was too sick to speak, until Commander Herid said slowly, "Young Van Stad is now in command. Said before he sent me off, in these clothes, with a hay cart, that those of us left have to stop wasting ourselves and concentrate on forming an effective resistance."

"King's alive, then?" Sereth persisted.

"Was when he sent us home." Commander Herid shut

his eyes, his lips a thin line, then he let out a breath and said, "King promised to escape, so they can't send him back a soul-bound ordering us to fight for them."

Sereth sat back, satisfied. He and the king are distant kinsmen, though I think they've met only once. "He's not stupid. He'll leave, and be back when he can do something for us."

"That's what he told us. Has to find some other rulers who know a lot of magic."

"What next?" I asked, more interested in our immediate future, now that I knew the king was safe.

"We wait. We're entirely at their mercy." I could see how he hated to say those words.

"Not completely. We can do something," I said, jumping up. "I'd best return. My foreigner mother will weep buckets, if it's known I'm out so late."

"Marend—"

"Yes?"

"It's my thought you'd best keep your distance from the garrison for a time. I don't know what's to become of us, or if the remedy to mind enchantment the king taught us some time ago will work. You and Retren might do best to lie low. See what they're like before doing anything."

"We'll see," I said, ignoring the blather about mind enchantments. Da had said most of it was mage-talk, no use to us.

I stealthed back in over the wall to the second story in case Mother was watching for me downstairs. I climbed in the library window and ran up to my room. Retren was there, asleep on my bed. I lit a candle, and the sound woke him up.

"Well?" he said.

"The royal city is lost. They killed the little princess. But the king escaped." I sat on the end of my bed, and began getting out of my wet clothes.

"What now?"

"Our resistance continues. But we'll add to the revenge for Da's death, vengeance for the Harskiald, and all the others at Aladas. We were too young to go to the royal city against them but we can make up for it by causing them as much trouble as we can, right here, with what's left of the group."

He turned his palm up in assent. "It's getting cold. Bet we'll get an early winter this year. Tchah! If they're coming, I hope they hurry because I want the revenge to start." He moved to the door. The shadows were dark there, but in spite of the tough talk his voice betrayed how much he was still missing Da, and all those at the garrison who were never coming back. "Oh—almost forgot..." He sidled a look at me so I knew what was coming before he said it. "Ramond sent a message. Wants to meet in the morning, about the Norsundrians. Calls a truce. Figures because of this we can forget—"

"I don't want to know what he says. Obviously he wants a truce or he wouldn't've sent a message."

"You don't need to be so nasty."

"It's that Ramond. Makes me that way, hearing his name. Where's the meeting at?"

"You'll go?"

"I'll think about it."

"The river gate, at dawn. If you don't go, I will."

"I said I'll think about it."

"I'll stop by here before I go. If we both go, we should together."

His last sentence was a change in tone (from challenge to suggestion) so I said, "Right."

He left quietly.

I flung the last of my wet things over a chair and climbed into bed. Ramond at dawn. Ugh. But it was better to face trouble than have it sneak up from behind. So I'd go. I'd decided to from the start, but Retren needed reminding of who was in command.

I woke up well before dawn and pulled on some clean clothes, then hesitated about last night's clothes. I can't stand any sort of mess in my room—even the lowliest guard at the garrison keeps his bunk area neat—but I'd also forbidden the servants to light my fire till it snowed. Before then, a fire was for weaklings. After, it just made sense. But my room was so dank and cold there was little use in spreading them out to dry. Finally I folded them and left them on the chair.

I put on riding trousers and sashed my shirt. I wore my usual long knife at my side, but put one of my short ones in my boot for just in case. I leaned out my open window. I breathed out. My breath was only a little bit visible. It had to be white for me to wear a coat.

I was just grabbing my bow to sling over my shoulder when Retren walked in. I couldn't see his expression in the gloom, but his shoulders relaxed a little bit so I could tell he was relieved.

"Ready?" he said.

"Yep."

We left.

We escaped the castle through the library window across the wall as usual. Mother wasn't likely to see us (she never emerged till midmorning) but it was easier.

"Want to take the shortcut?" Retren said, and pointed east, where the clouds showed an edge of light gray.

"No hurry," I said.

"It's dawn now. We've got half an hour to the river gate street."

"We do not answer a summons. He can wait."

Retren gave an impatient hop. "Bet he'll think we overslept, and we're soft."

I laughed. "If he could think that, he's a worse fool than I thought. Besides, it matters naught what he thinks of us."

"That's true." Retren brightened considerably.

"Did you bring a second knife?"

"Of course!" he said. "In my boot top. Doncha think he'll keep the truce?"

"Don't know. Since we've never had one before," I snarled, and he flushed. But it really was a stupid question.

Puddles lay in the streets, and the stones were cold through my boot soles. Winter *was* coming early this year. The streets were completely empty and dark. It was a strange feeling.

The river gate surmounted the high walls. We went the back way, and dropped onto the wall quietly through the (empty) guardhouse.

Two figures waited, facing east across the river. One was sitting on a battlement, the other standing leaning against it. Ramond was standing; I could pick out his stupid skinny body even in the gray half-light. They turned at our approach, when Retren's boots ground on the stone.

Ramond didn't move but the other pulled up his legs from where they were dangling fifty feet above the river, turned around and jumped down to stand beside his idiot friend.

Without saying anything, Ramond drew his dagger (he wasn't wearing a sword), laid it on the battlement his friend had just vacated, and stepped back, empty hands at his sides. His friend waited till I drew mine and I tossed it down near the other, careful (without showing it) they didn't touch. Retren and the Ramond-rat drew theirs, and dropped them.

Ramond was staring at me. I looked east, though I could see his movements out of my eye corners. "You called it."

"Your father's dead. There'll be no defense of the city," the friend spoke up, and I wished I hadn't spoken first. I felt the rat wanted to remind me of the defeat, as if Father's loss was my fault.

"Spit it out, or I'm gone."

Retren stood quietly beside me. I could feel him watching them intently. He twitched once and I was annoyed, and resolved to reteach him to relax: tensing up so much looks stupid, and when one needs to leap into action it makes for mistakes and jerky movements.

"Are you going to sit by and let the Norsundrians move in?" the boy said sharply. He looked my age.

"I don't see it's any of your business," Retren began.

"At least half of your group is gone. Only the babies are left." Ramond's glance flicked over Retren, who only twitched, I was relieved to note, and didn't give that the worth of a response. Then he looked back at me. "If we work in conjunction, we might be able to do something about the enemy."

Retren started to talk but Ramond half raised a hand. "I did not say with, I said in conjunction. With reasonable knowledge of each others' plans, we won't risk tripping over each other if we go for the same target."

I kept my hand on Retren's arm, and faced the east wall again. There was now enough light to see, and the roads were empty.

I turned my mind to the suggestion. It made sense.

"Possibly," I said. "How."

"Messengers."

"The castle is easily accessible, as you know, but I'm not familiar with your current hole," I said.

"A place can be arranged that is equally accessible to both sides."

"Meantime?" The rat looked puzzled. What a fool.

Ramond got it. "Truce. Leave one another alone, should contact occur."

Retren was tensing again and I pressed him very slightly. He relaxed again. I couldn't decide. The sense of it was warring with the strong feeling of NOT wanting to give up fighting Ramond's rats whenever we flushed one out. But—Da said tough decisions should take time in any but actual battle situations—

"I'll ask my friends," I said finally.

"Kethadrend will be here at dawn tomorrow to hear your choice. Whichever, we'll go from there." Ramond reached swiftly for their two knives. I was still and pressed against Retren's arm to keep him still: if they tried anything we were still armed, meanwhile we would not scramble.

Ramond tossed the rat his knife and they left. Kethadrend. I always note their names when I find them out.

Retren picked up our knives and handed me mine. We went back through the guardhouse and cut for home across the rooftops. He didn't speak till we were almost home. "I want to do it."

I could tell he was waiting for what I'd say.

"I really do want to talk to the others. I *don't* want a truce with them. It makes sense, but I don't know if we can trust him at all. Besides." I shrugged. "Working with them is a disgusting feeling."

Retren assented. "Well, I hope they come today. I want to get busy on the revenge."

"Me too." I said the obvious this once because it would make him feel better, about our father. But then I told him about those other things.

Two

WHEN WE GOT BACK to the castle, we separated and went to our rooms. I took off my knife in case there was a chance of Mother being up early, then ran down to see about breakfast since I hadn't eaten anything the day before.

The kitchen servants were all up and about. Most took no notice of me since they were used to my being in and out, and I required no ceremony or special service from them. I figure a warrior has to be self-sufficient. *Naturally* this was something else my mother disapproved of, but as it was mutually satisfactory (I also cleaned up after myself) the servants did not tell her.

As I was sitting at one of the carving tables and eating, I began to think about my mother's demands. All of them were senseless, and the way she'd enforced them before was to complain about me to my father. His method had been, tell me about each new demand, and beat me the second time I was caught ignoring it. We both knew it would happen and it was I who decided whether or not to risk it. But with Da gone—no more senseless rules. I wouldn't treat her badly (that was against my own rules) but the stupid stuff, no one could make me obey.

I finished my food and went up to the library to study a few more streets on the map. This was my newest project—I wanted to know the streets in Ramond's territory as well as I knew our part of the city so I would not be helpless anywhere I went.

I'd only been at it half a watch before Halan came in.

"Home today! The Jarlan wishes to see you."

"Thanks," I said.

"Wanted you last night," she said. This was a clue, so I thanked her again.

I first started for my room to change into my mother-clothes, then I remembered and laughed. I put my maps away and left.

My mother's rooms were at the northwest wing of the castle. She had them all tricked up with tapestries and plants and rugs and such foolery, and it always smelled of some sweet and heavy scent. I couldn't stand it there. She had the fires going, too, and I always felt like I was being smothered in a jewel box. I had this urge to get out as quick as I could.

One of her maids let me into her sitting room when I knocked.

"Is my mother out of bed?"

"No," the woman said in a hushed voice. "Please — she is still very upset."

I left her twittering behind me and went across to my mother's room, and opened the door myself.

She was lying on her foreign day couch with her hair carefully brushed and spread all over her fancy pillows and this robe thing on with embroidery and jewels. Her eyes were circled with dark skin, and puffy from weeping. When she saw me, she lifted one hand as though it were heavy as a sword, pointed vaguely in my direction, then dropped it.

I said before she could say anything, "You wished to see me, Mother?"

"Marend, how many times have I requested you not to wear those clothes?"

"Thousands, I'm sure," I said, still standing in the doorway — I wanted to make it short. "And Da beat me when you complained. Well, there's no one to do it now, and since you never once gave me any kind of reason besides looks, which I consider as contemptible a non-reason as you can think of, you're going to see 'em from now on, if you have to see me. Anything else?"

She blinked at me and wiped a hand across her eyes. I realized she was starting to weep and I was disgusted, but I didn't say anything.

"What could possibly interest you at the garrison, Marend? Or of war, for that matter? I understood how attached you were to your father, but—with—him—gone—" Her voice quavered, and I was so disgusted I could barely control it and I had to look away to make sure I had control of my expression.

Just then the door opened behind me, the sitting room-to-hall one. Naturally I kept still, but I recognized the footsteps of one of the maids and I was prepared to ignore her but then the rap of a man's boot heels followed.

"Jarlan?" the maid said behind me and I stepped inside the bedroom to let her pass and sneaked a look beside me without moving my head. I was completely unprepared to see Commander Herid—but I controlled it.

He looked at me carefully. His movements betrayed how uneasy he was in this smothering women's-den and I though briefly again how some adults (ones I really respected) had less control than I did. But then my father had once told me in private (and I had seen the evidence of it) that although Herid was a *good* teacher and an unsurpassed warrior, he was not much of a commander. Circumstances had placed him in command—he hadn't earned it. But I was training myself to command. Father told me when I was little that in order to command one must first learn to command oneself, which meant control. So maybe that was it.

Anyway I thought this as he walked across the room. When he saw her face he looked even more embarrassed.

"Jarlan—Good morning—" He made a salute only slightly awkward.

She smiled and put back a lock of her hair.

"Good morning, Commander Herid. How kind of you to come."

"I came to warn you of imminent danger, but perhaps Marend has already done that—"

She sighed. "I fear as usual Marend has told me nothing, beyond that now that Jarend is not here to enforce them, my wishes are to be completely ignored."

He looked from her to me, and shifted his weight like he was sitting on quicksand. Since she clearly expected him to say something, and I didn't lower myself to an argument on a dismissible subject. he said, "I was never aware that

Marend was a discipline problem."

"It's those clothes," she wailed.

He looked at me in surprise. He'd never seen me in anything else, of course.

I fought an impulse to laugh at the combination of their faces and the stupidity of the situation, and said with my best stoneface, "I have explained to my mother I see no reason to wear unpractical clothes, therefore I shall desist."

"You cannot wear — er — the ones you don't like just when you see your mother?"

"I see no reason to. After all, she does not — " (I did not say obviously) " — dress to please me."

"But *I* am your *mother.*" She dabbed at her eyes again.

"Marend," Herid said, "flouting the authority of your mother because she cannot enforce it is unfair. Hereto you have always obeyed orders — " He paused, and I saw the trap. He'd make it an order since I always respected garrison protocol: if I refused, saying I was not a recruit and he had no authority here anyway, then I would be told I had no place at the garrison, since I only "obeyed" what pleased me. Which was true, but it was my business to make sure *that* wasn't seen till I had some power of my own.

And he could tell I saw it. I berated myself for under-estimating them both. My mother had always had a way of getting what she wanted — a way I thought despicable but still a way. And he knew me better than anyone alive did. So I deserved the outcome.

"Very well: henceforth you will not see me in these." I did not add *you won't see me at all*, since I don't make threats to those with more power than I have. And I left. He could give her the news, and I had to meet with some of my group to discuss the Ramond problem.

That lackwit Ramond had been right when he said most of my gang was gone. Made up almost entirely of teens my age or near, many had run off, following the academy seniors who broke orders. Rumor was, Norsundrian archers used them as target practice.

At any rate there was a wretchedly depleted gathering in one of the old storerooms in the guard tower on the north wall. Present I had eight teens, and four of them had wrapped-up wounds — the Norsundrians had shot at us while we ran for bandages. Three of them were Retren's age and one was ten. I looked at the diminished number, at first as sick inside as when I found out about my father but I squashed it hard into anger, because anger is a fire. You can fight with fire, but tears are just sodden and do nothing.

Retren said as I crossed the room and sat on the windowsill, "Told them, Marend."

"What do you all think?"

They looked around. I watched the twins. The rest were followers, not thinkers. Tdor looked at Sindan, who said, "Tdor and I like it. Long's we don't have to do nothing with them."

"Rest of you?"

Palms up. Of course. The wildest among us had not come back.

Tdor spoke up. "So do we change the plans? We going go after the Norsundrians instead of the Ramond-rats now?"

"Both. If they give us *any* trouble. But if you scrap, don't leave them unconscious, I guess."

"Good!" she said. "Scrapping is good. Save the arrows for Norsunder."

"We will try it for a time," I said. "I want everyone vigilant. If the rats betray us once, or it seems they are allying with those Norsundrians, then we will make them targets. I don't know if the king will find out or not. We can assume he does, but if they kill any of us, then we've a right to fight back. We'll pass the word if we have any plans involving everyone."

I waited till they were all gone, then left. I wanted to get in some sword fighting practice before I hunted Norsundrians.

I found Sereth in the storage back room. He lowered his hands sharply and picked up a tray of dishes, then when he saw me, his shoulders relaxed. He set aside the tray, and brought out a bag of feathers, which I could see he was preparing for fletching. He sat on a stool, with his wounded leg set on a basket of summer uniforms.

I said, "I was hoping to get in some practice. Your leg too bad?"

"I can still make you sweat, standing on one leg."

The Norsundrians hadn't taken the wooden practice swords when they raided the garrison armory. Both Sereth and I needed to be moving, I would say. We kept at it until he was limping badly and my arm ached.

But night came, and to keep my mind from taking notice of the cold, I ran hard around the courtyard, top speed.

You can outrun cold, but you can't outrun thought. Memory. I got angry instead, at memories, emotions, all stupid, useless idiocy that interfered with your effectiveness in fighting. What *use* were emotions? Well, the ones besides determination, bravery, and resolution.

I concentrated on being resolute, and decided Ramond had come up with his blasted plan not so much to fight Norsundrians as to undermine my authority. And this I could not acknowledge to the others. I had to take their obedience for granted, or at least I had to seem to, or by fretting over it I'd lose in their eyes.

My object was to kill Norsundrians, protect my own authority, and if possible make Ramond look like the fool he was.

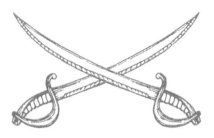

Three

BY THE TIME WINTER hit — and it hit Methden hard — I was well into a strategy.

I worked out my plans carefully, instructing my people just before I let the rats know what we were up to. I gave the sketchiest communications, ostensibly in case they fell into the wrong hands but actually so it appeared we were pulling off our complex plans lightning-fast, mostly raiding supplies, with an eye toward grabbing weapons. We also attacked couriers, and burned their messages, which were written in Norsundrian, so we couldn't read any of it. No way would Ramond's rats dare to horn in on our actions; meanwhile I was keeping my group in constant training so the differences between us and the rats would widen.

I was glad to see signs of heartening as the shock of grief began to wear away, and my gang started seeing improvement. They threw themselves into practice with fierce enthusiasm. This fostered the group identity again. I saw how very nearly it'd been shattered by the Norsundrians beating us. And so, with our proud identity intact, everyone — even my brother, who had tendencies toward softness — curled lips disdainfully at the rats' occasional suggestions we act together.

That brought us to the end of the year. The Week 'Tween was celebrated rather grimly by plans each day. Successful ones.

Until then we had what I realize in retrospect was a minimal Norsundrian presence. We hated them so much that the sight of any of them angered us; they had posted warnings everywhere that anyone seen with a weapon would be instantly shot. And they carried it out. They had, of course, gone through and taken every weapon they could find, but though we called them stupid, they were not stupid enough to think that they had gotten them all.

I kept my bow hidden in my wardrobe, within one of the long, embroidered robes my mother insisted I wear. So fitting, I thought. My arrows were stashed under the day lounger in Mother's room that smelled like flower perfume. I'd noticed the search was cursory there.

Ramond's group had some successes, I ought to report. It wasn't just us. Between our two groups, we did enough damage, especially bringing down roaming sentries and spies, that a new commander appeared in the bitter frost that greeted the new year. She began by issuing all manner of edicts, sanctions, curfews…to no avail. The fools had not yet stumbled onto the fact that we were teens; I felt badly that the adults, especially the mostly-healed garrison, couldn't scratch an itch without a patrol landing on them, but this was war.

A fresh wing of reinforcements was sent from the royal city. Chortling in triumph, we lay low to watch for a time. The old commander was yanked and a new one put in, who tightened things up with constant surprise searches and patrols at all hours, day and night.

They did not know our identities. My mother had unexpectedly provided me with a perfect cover: whenever the Norsundrian commander came to the castle to hand down his latest rules, she'd be sitting like a weepy, drooping flower. I'd be on a stool at her feet, the hated clothes strictly a disguise, and a bland, stupid smile on my lips. Lesra would be lumping about nearby, her sappy fair curls a match for my mother's.

The culmination of my hopes occurred well into winter. Ramond sent a message, and once more we met on the bridge wall, this time to look down on a cloudy-iced river. And we were both alone.

I had accepted only because I relished his having to admit my powers of command left his at the gate. And I let it show in my face when I stepped down onto the stone parapet and tossed my knife down. Excitement made me warm so I was only in shirt, breeches, and boots; I took one look at this thick well-made coat, the yeath-fur edged cap on his head, and transferred my gaze to the river. What a fool! A soft fool.

"Nollard says you and your group are starting to gamble on who can make the Norsundrians fall farthest when you shoot 'em," Ramond began, his round brown eyes curious.

"So?" I smiled just a little, and wished I'd allowed Retren to come, to enjoy our triumph. I hadn't — he'd managed to catch a cold, for which stupidly he had to stay at home. Our Da had said repeatedly that red noses and watery eyes were softness. Add to that, his noisy breathing and coughing might even bring death on us if the enemy heard.

"What d'you mean, *so*?" Ramond threw up his gloved hands in exasperation. "It's disgusting, that's what it is! I really think you enjoy all that killing!"

"I do. And so would you if any of you were good enough." And, and couldn't resist: "Not bad for babies, eh?"

He grimaced. "Why do I have the feeling talking to you is a big waste of time? Look, Marend." He threw out his hands. "I apologize for everything — everything! I'll take *all* the blame for *all* the problems, I promise. You can tell every teen in Methden if you want."

"Your tone says you're doing me a favor. Which you are not. The whole thing was your fault in the first place."

He sighed. "All right. I admit it! I was a big-mouthed, stupid nine-year-old. And the duel that got Lanrid and Hal killed, I claim my share of that. Somehow it was so easy to let tricks turn into topping, and topping into proving, and from there it's 'Oh, so *that's* the way you want it, I'll show *you*.' But — tell the truth — weren't you *glad* when the king said…no." He grimaced again. "I can see you weren't. You know, you've dressed like a Norsundrian for years, and now I think you're beginning to turn into one!"

I did not dress like a Norsundrian. They wore those gray tunic-jackets, and my clothes were stealth blacks, regulation at the academy. As Ramond well knew.

I did not deign to show by any sign that I had heard this pointless whining. "You're finished?" I said finally, after a protracted silence.

He turned around, shrugged, then turned again. "I must be. We seem to be speaking separate languages. You know, I thought our working in conjunction against a common enemy, a *real* enemy, would bring the feud to a close—*why* don't you believe me?"

I allowed my lip to curl. "What is this now, a ploy so I won't take over your group? I assure you I will not, because I don't need them, and haven't the time to train them."

He turned away, picked up his knife, jammed it in its sheath—I don't even think he was aware he'd done it. "How was I going to do that when I was supposed to start the academy this spring?—the *art* academy, up north."

I had to laugh. "You mean, you were rejected from the only academy that matters?"

He took a few steps away, then turned. "I had a place, but I went against the wishes of my father, my uncle, *your* father, Old Sereth—" He raised a hand and grimly ticked off the fingers. "I don't want to be a warrior. I never did! And I'm *going* to be an artist."

"What were you afraid of? I've seen worse recruits than you at the garrison!"

He looked amazed. "You just don't understand, do you? How would you like to be told you might be a good cook?" He jumped down and ran off.

I went home to report to Retren, Tdor, and Sindan, and I allowed myself to relish every detail.

And the next day I made a new acquaintance.

My mother was sent word that the commander and a guest were going to call on her. That meant Retren and I had to make an appearance—supposedly we were under house arrest. As I've indicated, I made certain I appeared for these calls to ensure my continued freedom; these were the only times my mother saw me.

I'd just sat down on my hassock and had received my mother's cloying smile when the visitors arrived. Lesra ignored them as she played with her dolls, and I affixed my stupid-face on, and laid my hands in my lap in a mindless pose.

The latest commander scanned us, his hawk's beak of a nose looking as usual as if he was sniffing out his opposition, if not his dinner, and next to his muscular bulk his companion appeared thin and flimsy. This fellow looked maybe ten years older than I (as opposed to the commander's middle age)—a new assistant? A desk jockey, perhaps? The thought of Norsundrian paperwork caused laughter to roil in my belly.

They sat down, and my mother made her usual pretense of being the Jarlan, and offered some refreshment. The commander refused cloddishly, as they always did, as if asked to perform a ritual. Maybe it is a ritual, I decided. The newcomer refused politely. Someone had stuffed the sort of outlander manners into him that my mother had stuffed into my unwilling ears.

I missed the introduction, which of course didn't bother me. I didn't think Norsundrians deserved names, and though I admitted to a mild interest in their system of promotions, they always spoke their detestable language so I'd discovered nothing about it.

The visit was fast. I was extremely annoyed when the commander asked Mother if the desk jockey could stay in the castle for a short time, as if they didn't already hold the entire garrison and all the outbuildings. And as usual, instead of standing up to him, she graciously extended our home to him as long as he wished to make use of it.

"Thank you, Jarlan," Skinny said. "I trust my business here in Methden will not occupy me long." The word *long* drifted on the air, and his eyes, which I saw were a bright shade of green, rested by chance on my face. My fatuous smile was firm, of course, but the amusement I saw in his expression invited me to share the joke. Naturally my face stayed flat and still and stupidly smiling.

The commander rose, and gave my mother a stiff jerk of his chin. The other bowed over her hand Toth-style and murmured, "I will let you know this afternoon where I will be ensconced. You may be sure it will be out of your way."

"How kind," she said. "Good morning."

Usually I followed right after, and went my own way, but I was so angry at her stupidity I *had* to speak.

"Mother, don't you understand they're placing a *spy* here?"

She opened her eyes at me, wide and sea-gray. "What would you have me do, Marend, bar the doors? Put a sword in Lesra's hands?" She smiled faintly, then said in her most wool-headed voice, "Personally, I rather like the idea of a spy wasting his time on my blameless life."

I snapped. "*I'd* be ashamed to face Da someday, and admit I'd done nothing. He despised cowardice more than *anything*."

She was looking droopy again, though there were no more tears. At least she'd stopped weeping publicly around the turn of the year. "If the king is alive, he will be back. He won't forget us. In the meantime, I believe my place is to preserve lives, and if by outward acquiescence I can do it, then I will."

It sounded like an excuse for cowardice to me, but at least it was a sign she had a plan. "He might be dead," I said. "And then it's going to be up to us."

"Sometimes..." She said even more softly, "I very much fear they allow trouble to go on just until they discover whether the causers are more bound up with the means than the end. I think they know that some...people...like those, would be the first to adapt to the Norsundrians' ways." She turned her eyes on me again, studying me carefully. I knew she couldn't read my expression—no one could unless I let them. I had worked hard on that.

"If you're worried about our people in the garrison—"

She sighed.

I ignored her, and continued. "Though they seem to exist with the Norsundrians they are *not* adapting. Those who have healed have to do all the household, stable, and equipment upkeep chores until they give parole. And none have, *that* I've been able to find out."

"Herid requested me last time he was allowed up here to see that you stayed away from the garrison."

"I have been. The Norsundrians won't let anyone around. Though I do keep an eye from a distance, or exchange a few words at the stable windows."

"Would you obey me if I forbid you to leave the castle at any time?"

"Of course not," I said coldly. "And if you try to force me, I'll disappear. I've things that must be done."

"Now, how am I going to force you?" She opened her hands. "Request the Norsundrians to act as my allies?

Herid didn't want you around because it further demoralized the warriors."

"I figured," I admitted reluctantly. "No one came to talk to me much when I did catch sight of 'em, except Sereth. So." I crossed my arms. "You can rest assured I've very little to do with the garrison." I wasn't about to tell her anything about what I *was* doing. "In fact, *none* of my friends go near it. No one appeared for Recruit Week this year. 'Course, I don't think the Norsundrians even knew about it, so it wasn't much of a back of the hand."

"Listen, Marend." She faced me. "I haven't asked if you know about the trouble in the city because if they send one of their mind-readers down I don't want information taken from me that I didn't approve of in the first place. I sense they are waiting, and are going to pounce on the ringleaders whenever they wish."

I shrugged. And left, when Lesra wandered in.

I went to my room to change into decent clothes. Retren was there, waiting.

"Where were you?" I said.

"Out spying."

"Find anything?"

"Nah. You?"

"They're moving a spy in. He looks and acts like a desk jockey, but…" I frowned, remembering how he'd smiled at me. None of them had ever deigned to notice me before — as it should be. "Keep an eye out. Green eyes, light brown hair kind of long. Civvies. *Might* not be as stupid as he looks."

Retren showed me his palm in agreement.

"Meanwhile, Mother inadvertently warned me. Thinks it's possible they're letting us hone ourselves — and then they'll come after us. I must admit their lack of retaliation this past month has had me uneasy. Well. We're going to call the gang together and have a talk on tightening up. No more carelessness! Honed we may be, we're *not* going to get caught! Put out the word."

"Usual time, place?"

I signed assent and he sighed softly.

"You know why we meet at midnight, Retren."

"I know. To combat softness. I just don't see why it seems so easy for you. I do what you do, and work as hard as you do, and I'm *cold – all* the time! Did you get sick when you were ten?"

"I don't get sick. Just as Da did not get sick. It's a matter of will. Your attitude must be at fault. Your senses must be made to work for you, or you'll end up serving them."

He squared his shoulders and turned to go. "I suppose I should skip dinner again tonight?"

I hesitated. I'd been toughening myself up by the time I was nine—here he was, near eleven, and I was still making the decisions. "You must determine that for yourself," I said finally. "You cannot rule others well if you cannot rule yourself. I too have smelled that chicken pie baking. If it intrudes on my thoughts too much today I will better school myself in the future if I skip it."

"It's just I'll feel sicker, I always do when I skip—I know," he raised a hand, "I know. I'm not concentrating enough." He sighed, and left.

It was just before dinner that I found out that the new Norsundrian had chosen Da's rooms in the tower. No one had disturbed those rooms since he was killed, and to have some enemy fool fumble in airily and decide, "Yes, this'll do," enraged me more than anything had since Da was killed.

"Yes, this'll do," he'd said to Mother's servants, and they'd meekly shifted the furniture around to his satisfaction. I would have died first. When he was settled, they were dismissed, and word had soon filtered through the entire castle. Mother had shut herself in her rooms again.

My mind seethed with plans for murdering that horseapple for daring to defile my father's place. I had sworn to myself that no one would set foot in them, *no one*, not even if I came into power. I was so angry my fingers ached to close around a knife. Scant relief was afforded me through lingering daydreams about assassinations, about scouring the room clean with his blood, and so forth.

If I were to do anything this violent, I knew I had to do it alone. But how? Anything I did would lay suspicion directly on my family's heads. I couldn't trust my mother or Halan or even Lesra not to give away clues to our identities if they were questioned as roughly as people had been early on in the investigation.

I could do nothing but curse impotently.

That is, directly. Skinny must be left to sit up there unmolested, but I would engineer a suitable response for his cohorts.

Concocting a plan eased that pain in my guts enough so I could sleep, and the next morning I called another meeting, and outlined my plan.

Tdor met it with loyal enthusiasm. A couple of the others seemed dubious and subdued. Retren stood looking like a stuffed fish, with his pale cheeks and red nose. I heard him coughing as soon as the door was shut behind him, on his way to deliver my message to the rats.

Four

THE ROYAL CITY COURIER was due to arrive. The courier was usually accompanied by five or six outriders.

We ghosted up to the old wall left from centuries ago, and shot them all as soon as they were within sight of the garrison, before they reached the north-gate bridge. I'd had my gang practice all the previous day, so we wouldn't have any embarrassing muffs. And it worked beautifully. I did not even need my second arrow, which I'd readied as soon as I gave the signal by downing my target. She tumbled off her horse and lay still. Spang! Spang! Ziss! Everyone's shots hit the targets, and I was pretty sure mine was dead.

Then began the difficult part, slipping away. They'd know the shots came from the other side of the canal, and they could have they area cordoned off for a house-to-house search very quickly.

They did. But we melted away along our arranged route, two large rain pipes being crucial to our descent. No one could see them from below. It was great knowing the city so well. How I laughed to myself as I climbed up to my room. I hoped that if ghosts were real, my father had seen *that!*

Next morning Halan came in to lay the fire. I was already up, doing my exercises, though the sun had barely lifted the eastern darkness. I'd been too excited to sleep. "I won't have one today," I said.

She picked up her basket of materials again, started out, then stopped. "That may be, but your brother needs one. He's sick."

"It's a matter of mind," I said coldly. "And he can do

what he wants."

"He follows your lead. And if it was just a matter of mind no one would ever get sick."

"My father taught me differently."

Her thin lips parted as if she was going to speak, but instead she walked out, shutting the door quietly behind her.

Next watch, one of the servants found me in the library. It occurred to me to do some reading about the Norsund-rians, as in "know your enemy." It was slow going, leafing through books, looking for information.

Anyway, a servant of Mother's appeared. "The Norsundrian has sent for you."

"Where is he?" I demanded, my anger over my father's rooms' defilement flaring.

"Your mother's morning room."

My anger intensified unexpectedly at this incursion into *our* domain. Unless she had invited him?

I made the servant wait while I changed, and after she went in I had to stop outside Mother's room to make sure my stupid-face was in place. I smoothed my hands down the front of my mother-clothes, to dry my palms. I was furious at them both, but I was not going to tip my hand by showing it.

I opened the door, and I saw instantly by my mother's excessively polite posture that she had not requested the interview.

My mother's head turned. "Ah. Here. You may ask Marend yourself. And if you desire to speak to Retren I believe I will request you to go to him. I understand he is in bed, sick."

The servant who'd bent to whisper to her left the room noiselessly.

Despite my mother's formal pose, the Norsundrian was seated comfortably, and somehow conveyed an air of being much entertained. "What can you tell me about last night's gesture, Marend?"

"Last night? Gesture?" I repeated stupidly.

"Everyone knows about it by now." His tone was gently chiding, as though he knew all about us.

Though my face stayed firmly fixed—I'd practiced too

long to lose it—my mind was off-balance from this unexpected response. Then I thought, it's just a pose. If this fool really knew, we'd all be up against a wall by now.

I said, "Somebody shot some Norsundrians, I heard. But why is that a 'gesture'?"

"Because," he explained with pleasant patience, "when people wish to obtain information, they usually arrangs to waylay couriers in some lonely location, and they never forget to take the dispatch bag. Last night's ambush was useless except as a gesture. No one attempted to relieve the courier of her bag, and the incident was executed in full view of the tower guards, most of whom were looking inward at the time. A problem that will shortly be addressed. This was a gesture somewhat in the nature of throwing down a war pennant, I believe." And he looked at me expectantly.

Danger prickled the back of my neck.

"I didn't hear anything," I said.

"Very well." He stood up. "Come, take me to your brother's room."

My mother's lips tightened slightly, but she didn't move, even when he wished her a good day. I stood up, and found that the Norsundrian was taller than he appeared while sitting down. Hatred surged. I blamed my mother for my lack of stature, and I disliked anyone who towered over me, which Retren soon would do—we were nearly eye to eye now.

But I forced myself to walk sedately, and I kept my gaze on the floor.

He asked, "Will you give me a tour of the castle, Marend?"

"Why don't you ask one of the servants?" I retorted, and immediately wished I'd said nothing.

"Are you too busy?"

That knowing tone was back in his voice. Was he goading me out of mean Norsundrian habit? I said sheepishly, "No, I'm not. But I've never gone up into the high parts. All I know is our wing, and I thought a servant might be able to give you a better tour. Here." I prevented him from answering by saying that last word a trifle abruptly, and I opened Retren's door.

Relief and irritation warred in me. Relief was foremost.

My brother was indeed in bed, a roaring fire heating the room, and a huge coverlet lying at the foot of the bed. He'd been staring into the fire.

His eyes turned to us. It was partly the leaping firelight and partly fever that made them appear so dark they were almost black, and glittering queerly as they shifted between me, the Norsundrian, and me again. He lay very still, the fever distorting his color so much (cheeks red, the rest blanched) it was hard to interpret his expression.

The Norsundrian said nothing. When the silence grew protracted, I turned his way, to discover him studying us both. He gave me that sharing-the-joke smile again and then stepped past me into the room.

Retren's gaze went to him, watchful, as he stepped to the bed. The Norsundrian surprised us both by reaching down and laying his palm across Retren's forehead. "You're sick indeed," he said, straightening up. "You'd do best to confine yourself to quarters for a few days." And he turned toward the door.

Was that a threat, or just fatuous advice? Retren looked to me for cues, then the Norsundrian said, "Don't you think?"

Retren swallowed, said hoarsely, "I've no wish to go anywhere."

"Sleep well," the Norsundrian replied, and went out.

Retren and I exchanged grimaces. I hung back, wondering if that cloth-head was expecting me to prance all over the castle with him, but he only murmured, "I expect we'll be conversing again shortly, Marend," and he started back down the hall. I waited until I knew he was around the corner, then I shut Retren's door.

"I'm sorry," he whispered unhappily. "It came on in the night. I just can't breathe, and I'm so dizzy when I stand up—"

"Don't apologize to me," I said curtly. "If you wish to grow up a weakling that's your affair. What did you make of *that*?" I jerked my head toward the door.

"Weird—" He swallowed. "Why'd he come here? With you?"

I gave him a succinct account of the interview in Mother's morning room. Then I finished, "In some ways he seems like less of a threat than the previous birdwits who've been in command here. But in other ways I feel there might be real danger. Or. The danger might from whoever is behind that fool."

"Should we back off? That pennant business worries me a little."

"Worries!" I repeated scornfully. "That's what it was supposed to do. I was just surprised they'd pick up what we meant."

"What?"

"What do you mean, what?"

"The pennant business is supposed to worry us?"

"No! Well, yes, actually, but I *meant*, we did it to mean exactly what he said!"

He frowned, and his head fell back on the pillow. "I'm sorry, Marend, I just can't seem to follow. What do you mean?"

I sighed. "And you're always complaining how I don't consult you enough, how I make all the decisions! How are *we* supposed to figure out what to do if you can't think?"

"I don't know." He turned his head, eyes shut. "Why don't you spy on him. You're sure to figure him out that way."

"I was intending to," I said. "I'll get to work." And, when he didn't answer, I mocked the Norsundrian's voice, "Sleep well!"

I left, deciding to ignore Retren for a full day. Not knowing what was going on would get him on his feet faster. And I needed to plan.

I decided to sound out Tdor. She often had excellent ideas.

She wasn't in the store, so I left our signal and faded more carefully than usual up to our usual hideout, a corbel in a corner where Wind-Street houses and west-bridge met, which couldn't be seen from any of the near windows.

I stared down into the dark, frozen water of the river, making and discarding plans. She was with me before too long, clambering up quickly, and flashing me an apologetic roll of her eyes. "Sorry, Marend, I had six deliveries. Sindan was inside."

"Wanted to talk to you. Something odd. Calls for careful movement."

She grinned in pleasure as she brought her bony knees

up under her chin and hugged them, her thin arms crushing her freshly starched apron.

I told her about the day's activities. She listened, her brow furrowing when I got to Retren's fever. She made a sympathetic murmur, and I said, "I am sorry too, but it's best if we don't show it. He's got to want to get rid of that cold. Our father said that time after time."

Tdor turned up her palm. "You know him best, but he almost fainted last night. I know he was trying hard. *No one would want to fall off a roof, and he almost did!*"

I hadn't known that. He'd kept it quiet. "But he didn't fall. That proves it's a matter of will," I said. "Now. Tell me your impressions concerning this Norsundrian."

She wrinkled her nose. "Sounds like a desk jockey to me. But whose words is he mouthing? I mean, what's the plan? Maybe one of us'd better try some spying down at the garrison, though it's absolutely crawling with the enemy. Maybe even try to lift any written orders the new commander's made, or at least listen to him talk."

"Good idea. But I'll do that. Why don't you get Sindan, maybe Harec or Lemarden to follow a few Norsundrians today. See if they talk about or do anything unusual. And we'll meet tomorrow."

She scrambled up and shook out her robe. We parted.

I did not want to admit to myself, much less out loud, that I didn't want to spy on the strange Norsundrian because I did not want to go near my father's room. I didn't see this as cowardice, or I'd've been sleeping up there every night since his death, Norsundrian or no Norsundrian. There was nothing to be *afraid* of. But it seemed somehow a dishonor to him. And it caused a curious pain I could not explain, or purge, except by avoiding his things. The Norsundrian being there intensified this feeling of trespass.

I examined my thoughts, looking for cowardice that I could pounce on and expunge. I couldn't find any, so I veered between impotent anger and bafflement.

I couldn't discuss it with Retren until he toughened his will. He'd even admitted he couldn't think properly.

I wasted the afternoon and part of the evening skulking about the garrison. About all I can say is, I remained unseen. The few times I heard anyone talk, it was in their language. I never saw Skinny the desk jockey — if he reported in that day, it must have been before or after he was annoying us.

I decided to vent my feelings in a plan. I had to: kill as many of them as possible; do some damage; and not reflect on any Methden citizens, while not exposing us. The usual, but my concentration was really on the first two.

My decision was intensified when both Sindan and Tdor appeared the next day, and reported that as far as any of them could ascertain, the Norsundrians behaved exactly as usual. Which I interpreted as ignoring us.

"You know," I said, "it's weird. They were slaughtering us when they invaded, then shooting us after. But now…now it feels like the stillness before a storm, in a way."

Sindan shifted. "Marend, two of the rats stopped in and offered their help. Said they're bored. That Keth, he's all right."

"No rats. We're tight and good. Don't need infiltration problems. Especially not now."

"I get the feeling their group has disintegrated."

"We'll see. I'll check it out, *after* we solve the problem before us now. This is what I have in mind. We'll feint 'em twice, then strike for real when they have two patrols in search. This time we'll attack the garrison itself…" and I went into the details: at midnight on the target day Rom and Harec were going to set fire to the south-gate guardhouse, making as much noise as possible, then Sindan and Lemarden were going to fire the garrison hay storage barn just outside the West Gate, with a flaming arrow, which we'd soak with oil the night before.

Lemarden would lead the search party into the warren of narrow streets in old-town, and Sindan would come to back us up.

So it went from our end, but their reactions were not their customary ones. When the patrols found the bluffs, they sent word to the main garrison, but the runners did not come back out with search patrols.

Nothing occurred at all. Once again my neck gripped with that danger sense.

Sindan finally appeared at my shoulder, and I asked, "What happened? Trouble?"

"No, went off without a hitch," he whispered back in surprise.

I assessed the main courtyard. From my hiding place in a crook between the city wall and a roof I could see a good portion of it, and the army side of our castle. Including my father's tower, which was dark and silent.

Then, quietly, Norsundrians began filing into the courtyard. There was a brisk flurry of activity as weapons and horses were issued…

But something was wrong.

I realized they were taking too long; I'd seen them pour out, pulling on swords and coats and mounting horses in one smooth motion, previously.

A stall? Sharply, quickly, I looked around—and I saw a man-sized shadow pass over the bridge wall onto a roof.

Were we being surrounded? One arrow would give away our position.

For the first time I raised my hand in the signal to abandon mission and decamp.

We all got away. I made sure the last of us were gone before I left, but I was shaken enough to take a very torturous route to the library window. I even listened outside my silent room before slipping in.

By morning my relief had turned perplexity, followed by frustration. I was in the midst of preparing another plan when my door opened and Retren walked in slowly. He moved toward the fireplace, blinked at its empty darkness, and collapsed into the chair as though his legs couldn't hold him. I noticed with dissatisfaction he was wearing two winter-tunics, laced tightly up to his throat. And a shirt underneath!

"Didja d-do something last night?" he quavered, then gave this low, cracking cough.

I eyed him, then relented. He *had* gotten up, at least. I gave him a report, but just as I finished Halan appeared at my door. She frowned at us. "You're to be in bed, Jarlan's orders," she said to Retren. "We're supposed to tell her when you're not."

Retren struggled up from his chair, held onto the back of it, and coughed. "Let me know…" He waved, and another paroxysm shook him. He left and I heard that low, wet crackle clear out in the hall.

Five

SKINNY THE DESK JOCKEY didn't come around that day, though I wore my mother-clothes in case. I impatiently let a night go by without doing anything, and we tried again. In fact, we tried three more times.

I kept getting that sense something was wrong, that we might be walking into a trap, and worse, that I was being watched. It'd be tripped by noticing the Norsundrians weren't where our estimates had placed them. They always had been before.

Each time I got that slugs-crawling-down-my-spine sense and made the abandon sign. Then I waited in a defeated fret until everyone had drifted down one alleyway or another, on their way home, before I slunk back to my room.

After three failures, followed by three sleepless nights imagining how my father would scorn me for cowardice, I determined to go ahead no matter what. I just couldn't bear Methden thinking we'd slunk away to our holes like Ramond's rats had.

I left the castle and went alone to meet the others because I'd banned Retren from participating until he got over that coughing.

I won't bother outlining my plan since it was a disaster from the beginning. We were going to attack the garrison, of course. And just before I was to give the signal (by shooting the gate guard, this time), once again I got that sense of watching eyes.

I lowered my bow and took my time scanning the

familiar night-dark buildings. Nothing. Anywhere. My father's tower was still dark.

I raised my bow, and began to track the guard. He appeared briefly, neck, chest and shoulders as he passed crenellations. I tightened my grip and willed the feeling to go away but it did not. Had I looked thoroughly?

Of course...

No, I hadn't.

My fingers clenched when once again my gaze swept past my father's tower and began to examine the adjacent walls. I was stupid enough to not want to look there?

Even with my bow raised, and my eyes tracking the guard, I could not resist one more check. My gaze flicked back like probing a sore to my father's office window, where we had spent so many agreeable hours talking and watching drill in the courtyard below. I forced myself not to look away, but scrutinized that window.

There was a silhouette a shade darker than the darkness. It was a man's silhouette. Very still. Watching. I knew it—he—was watching.

I froze.

The silhouette shifted. Faint light leaked from somewhere behind him, no more than a thin line marking the contour of a shoulder, a light-colored shirtsleeve, cheekbone, jaw.

I whipped the bow up, and released the arrow. The figure vanished from sight a heartbeat before the arrow zipped through the office window.

I took a deep breath. "I was spotted," I said to Rom and Sindan, who were nearest me. I could feel their surprise. "Go home and hide out till you hear from us. Now." I added as silent Norsundrians came out of the barracks, some to the gate, and some to the bridge.

I didn't go in the easy library-window way, but climbed up through my bedroom window across my balcony, so I could check the room first. No one there! Rejoicing in my dark hair and night-black clothes, I hid my bow away, threw my clothes under the bed, and climbed in bed wearing my singlet and drawers, as usual. I even ducked my head under the pillow and lay utterly still, thinking: *if* anyone sticks their head in the door I'll look asleep.

And not two turns of the small glass later was startled into a flinch I couldn't control when a cold hand smacked my shoulder.

I flung my pillow away and yanked my arm aside to stare up into a night-shadowed Norsundrian face. "Get dressed and come with me," he said.

"The Jarlan of Methden's children are *not* in the habit of being disturbed at night. We wait on our *own* convenience," I said loftily. "Come back if you must in the morn—"

"You have the count of ten to get something on," he said, and walked away to the door, keeping his back to me.

Speechless with rage at being ordered about, and at being in such a stupid position (from now on, I vowed, I sleep fully clothes except for boots) I grabbed my stuff from under the bed, yanked on the trousers, and even as I pulled the tunic over my head I was running for my open window.

He must have heard my footsteps; he crossed the room in three steps, and hard fingers wrenched my arm as I got one foot over the sill. I brought up my knife, shook it free of sheath and belt, and attacked. My first real hand-to-hand fight! Exhilaration coursed through me when I saw an unmistakable jerk of surprise. He raised an arm to block and I feinted, switched hands, drove it upward—and lost momentum when that other hand on my arm yanked me off balance.

Cursing, I braced my feet and twisted violently, nearly freed myself, brought up the knife—and was surprised by a painful explosion of lights as a fist I never saw socked me. I hit the floor hard. A foot planted in my back, my flailing hands were grabbed, yanked up behind me, then tied.

The Norsundrian hauled me up by my collar and dumped me ungently on my feet. Rage as well as that tight grip nearly strangled me. He kept his fist firmly on the scruff of my tunic and marched me up the back way to my father's tower. As soon as I saw it, sick dread mixed with grief. This was not my choice. I resolved not to show weakness.

I got shoved through the door. The room was not the same. The familiar furniture had been disturbed: the desk was against the other wall, the two plants in their ancient pots were gone, and other little things out of place. And worst, instead of my father looking up from the desk to smile at me that tall Norsundrian was lighting a second lamp.

The window was still open to the air.

He set the lamp on a side-table with neat stacks of papers. The Norsundrian let go of my collar and shoved me further into the room. I stumbled, caught myself, and heard the door shut behind me.

"Sit down, Marend."

"You may's well stick me in your dungeon, or whatever you're going to do, because I'm not going to rat on anyone, or tell you anything."

He sat down in a chair, made a little gesture that I almost missed, and the cord disappeared from my wrists. *Disappeared*. A power gesture. *Ignore*, I told myself. I realized my wrists hurt and I rubbed them as I sat down.

"That remains to be seen," he replied, looking amused. "As yet, I might add, I have no interest in your friends."

I was braced for threats of torture, including the torments of my friends to force me to do Norsunder's will. This statement surprised me so much I exclaimed, "Then why didn't you wait to harass me until morning?"

He smiled. "Because I have pressing business elsewhere in the morning. In fact, enough business in other places to keep me away for some little time. Therefore I believe it is necessary for us to come to some sort of understanding before I go."

"*Understanding*—?" I repeated, outraged. "D'ya think I'm a collaborator? If so, you're stupider than I thought! Who *are* you, anyway? Nothing you do or say makes any sense. Are *you* a collaborator? If so, then that'd explain a fatuous belief that *I'd* ever become one!"

"I thought I introduced myself to you and your family. My name is Imry Llyenthur. The question of collaboration is, ah, an interesting one. We will have to debate the meaning once we get a bit more leisure time."

I waved my hand, dismissing him and his name. "*That* tells me *nothing*," I said scornfully, aware that I'd always imagined if I got caught I'd be scared, or terrorized, or bored, or numbed, but *never* that I'd have fun mouthing off. They actually sent a desk jockey! I settled in to enjoy myself.

"What is it you wish to know?" He put up his brows. "Who my father was? Where I was born—"

"What's your rank? Are you the latest fatwit comm- ander's assistant?"

"You might say he's mine," the Norsundrian respond- ed mildly, which effectively destroyed my enjoyment. I began to get an idea that I was much less in control of Methden—of my future—certainly of the situation, than I'd started out thinking.

"Rank," he went on, folding his hands. "That is another matter for debate. I'm not particularly interested in titles, but in, ah, let's call it success. My minions are very strongly encouraged to strive for success." He wiggled his brows, threat disguised as humor.

Astonishment made me stare stupidly, "Then it's *you* in charge."

"To a degree." He turned up his palm. "Certainly here in Marloven Hess. Do you have any more questions about my credentials?"

It finally sank into my brain that all my plans, obser- vations, and exercises, had availed me nothing. I was walking dead, and only my pride kept me from giving any hint of the sudden, overwhelming dejection that flooded my mind. Da, here I come, on your heels, and you'll just be ashamed because I was a failure after all.

"I've heard enough." I forced myself to shrug. "What now, a suitable execution?"

"Try to disabuse yourself of the notion we employ the majority of our hours arranging public executions. Not that they don't have their place. They can be very effective as well as entertaining—"

"You can't make me go Norsundrian any other way!"

"Actually, we can, with this." He flexed his hand, and a dagger dropped into it from his loose sleeve. The unex- pectedness of it made my stomach knot. "I have only to put your name on it, as we say. There is a problem with that, though: in order to make the effect, ah, effective, it takes time. That, I don't have."

I was determined not to show any relief. I gave him the fatuous court face Mother had forced me to learn, which caused that familiar smile to narrow his eyes. He slid the knife back into the wrist sheath, but I did not relax. "Which brings us to you. Much as I'd like to converse further, I have to be somewhere by the next watch bell, and I don't foresee returning for some days."

Then...prison? Dungeon? *Death?*

"This country has a large number of orphans, most of them well trained, and you might be useful in an experiment I plan to set up."

An *experiment?*

"More of that later. Right now, in order to establish peace in Methden I have to curtail your activities. You have a choice before you, therefore. Either give me your word you'll stay in the castle, or I'll have to find a suitable lockup. Which won't be in Methden. Mmight not even be in the country."

"Just—stay in the castle?"

He laughed. "Your friends can visit you as they please. I should mention, though, that there won't be any sanctions against shooting them. The only ones with any potential yet are the greengrocer twins, but I have no real necessity for them as yet, so if you have any regard for them you might encourage a hiatus."

He paused long enough for me to comprehend the fact that he was better informed about my gang—at least two of them—than I'd assumed, then added, "One of the things I find so disappointing about you Marlovens is your leaning toward lighter hypocrisy. I suppose you're worried how it will look if you take the sensible course?"

"All right," I said shortly. "I'll stay in the castle."

"Excellent." He smiled at me. "Remember the idea was to curtail your ambush-activities, so I will regard shooting people from inside the castle windows, for example, as a breach of parole."

My eyes involuntarily went to the window. He saw my glance, stood up, and went to the desk. "Here." He came back with my arrow. "You'll get to use it again." He put it into my hands. "I'll talk to you when I get back."

I jumped up from my chair and left very swiftly. There were no Norsundrians. The halls were deserted. Clutching my arrow, I began to run.

I got to my room, and lit a candle. The covers were still rumpled on the floor. My knife belt lay by the window where I'd dropped it, my knife nearby. I looked around, feeling the whole incident had been unreal. I looked at the arrow in my hands, evidence that it had happened.

I left. Retren was asleep, but woke quickly enough when I shook him. Though his fire had died his floor was still warm. It was a relief to my bare feet after the icy halls and my icy room.

"Wha—Marend?" He coughed, choked, sat up, and fumbled for a handkerchief, which he coughed and honked into.

"When you've finished your edifying performance," I said, using Da's old phrase and voice when we'd cried or whined, "I'll tell you what happened."

"Sorry." He swallowed a cough. "Light a candle so I can see you. Did you do a plan? Did it work?"

"A disaster. And I got caught," I said as I lit a candle.

"What? Why're you carrying an arrow?"

"Oh—" I realized I still held it, and threw it down. "Listen." I told him what happened. He frowned, listening without saying a word. At the beginning he stifled a yawn so hard his eyes watered—by the end, the yawns were gone.

When I finished, "That's horrible," he said, his voice still gravelly. "What're we going to do?"

"I don't know. We'll have to think on it, I guess. I was wrong about so many things—imagine! He even knew who Sindan and Tdor are, though he says he doesn't want them yet. I wonder what his experiment is?"

"Who cares?" Retren squeaked. "Whatever it is, it's still Norsundrian stuff!"

"What're you moaning about? I didn't say I approve, or that I will cooperate, I'm just interested in finding out why he's picked me out from the gang, and what he thinks I can do."

Retren shook his head slowly.

I said with extreme exasperation, "Do you fear that *I* am weak-willed enough to betray Marloven Hess after just talking to this fool?"

"All I hear is, you're talking like you're considering it if you want to know what it is. It's Norsundrian stuff, Marend. It doesn't matter what it is—it's *all* evil!"

"Considering? Oh, the horror! Don't be more stupid

than you can help. It's *always* best to know your enemy; he certainly seems to know plenty about *us*. I think it's an excellent opportunity to gain first-hand information while he's willing to blab on and on. Gathering information is not *switching sides*, or there'd be no spies! I'll just be *spying*, Ret. Besides, what else can I do? I promised I won't make any attacks, and if I break my word I'll be like *them*. Do you," I said acidly, "think I should have picked being stuck in a dungeon in some other country?"

He hunched his shoulders. "I don't know what's right," he said morosely. "I guess you should be spying, but you shouldn't be showing any interest in what they'll use you for if they talk you into turning against us—"

"You may tell me what I *shouldn't* do," I said coldly, "when you're smart enough, and strong enough, to lead us."

"Well—look where *you* led us!" He pointed to the arrow. "And things've turned out so different, so *weird*, from what we suspected—expected, I mean—I think you should be careful!"

"I intend to be careful," I said, "and to give him as little valuable information as possible. He's a blabber-mouth. Do you know, *I* asked more questions than he did. And *he* told me everything I wanted to know!"

"Da once told me asking questions gives the answerer information."

"He'd never say something so clumsy."

Retren grimaced. "Ah, you know what I mean! When he said it, he meant he liked the questions I was asking when we were talking about history."

"So you're saying, the Norsundrian let me ask questions to find out what I'm interested in."

"Could be."

"All right, that's something to consider." I frowned, thinking over the interview. "What did he learn... He won't get the impression I'm soft. And he *will* get the impression I don't think much of them. Why don't you go out at dawn. Tell the gang to meet here. I'd better hold a meeting."

"I don't know if—" He stopped, coughing. "Sure."

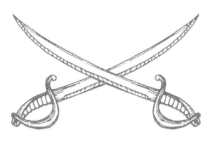

Six

WE MET THE NEXT night, in the library. I knew there was no danger of any of the family or servants eavesdropping, and as for the Norsundrians, who knew about them anymore? I could see this same question in the others' faces. I caught both Retren and Rom sidling glances at the door and window from time to time.

When I had given them a complete account of the interview, they sat in silence. After a long pause I said, "So? What d'you think?"

Tdor said, "I don't know what to think. They know me'n Sindan, huh?" She pursed her lips. "The shooting threat doesn't bother me nearly as much as their knowing about us all along. We've expected to be shot at while in action, but we also expected to remain anonymous."

"Yep." Sindan snapped his palms up in agreement, as usual—he almost always echoed whatever Tdor said. "What d'we do now? Pull off a plan and risk being pincushions, while Marend lurks around here?"

"We need Marend too much," Tdor said emphatically. "We need *all* our brains working. One thing is plain. If we haven't exactly underestimated them, we *have* figured 'em wrong. Maybe we'd do better if we wait till Marend's got some more info out of that Imry Llyenthur character, and we can go from there."

"Our strategy's been poor anyway," Retren croaked suddenly. "Time we reassessed. Form a new one."

I frowned. "You've never questioned it before. In fact you agreed with the strategy before."

He looked down at his hands. His posture, his voice told me he'd been given new "insight" — and it was more than a chance he'd gotten it from someone I disapproved of. "If you've decided to stop loafing and start working, we're *all* pleased! And likewise, if you've suddenly gained powerful wisdom, we are waiting for enlightenment," I said as sarcastically as possible.

"It was my fault," Lemarden said suddenly, looking acutely uncomfortable. "We didn't *mean* to talk to the rats. I got mad when Retren came this morning, and I thought the Norsundrians'd got the info from the rats, and I ran out, and since Kethadrend lives two streets over, I went there."

"By the time I caught up they were fighting," Retren added, wiping his nose.

"I attacked first, no questions." Lemarden grinned.

"I couldn't stop 'em," Retren went on, and flushed when I curled my lip at him. "I guess his sister went to find someone to stop it, and Ramond and his cousin Nollard came, with Keth, and pulled us apart, and sat on us both. Wanted to know how it started."

"Wouldn't let me up unless I told 'em. So I told 'em."

"And I had to tell 'em more to set the facts straight."

"Which means the rats know I'm stuck here?" I sighed. "You birdwits! They were the *last* who should have found out, can't you *see* that?"

There was silence, then Retren said in a mumble, "Anyway it was Kethadrend said our tactics were good, execution excellent, but strategy stupid. What's more, now't I see it, I agree."

"Our strategy," I reminded him coldly, "was simply to kill Norsundrians, and to keep the rats from infiltrating and taking over our group."

"There's been no danger of that for weeks." Retren shrugged.

"We knew that, and the rest was so much fun, we kept on. So what?" Tdor said briskly. "If we want to change, we change! Meanwhile, *I* think the rats are secondary to the Norsundrians. What do we do? I vote like I said before, wait for Marend to pump this birdwit for more info!"

I was so angry with Retren for discussing me behind my head, then undercutting my command, that I couldn't think; Tdor's sensible talk reestablished my charity. I gave her a smile, and she grinned back.

The rest agreed. They soon left, and Retren started out without a word.

"Retren, I want to talk to you."

He swung around. "You can jaw at me tomorrow," he croaked. "I'm going to bed!" he added in a defiant tone. "I know I'm soft, and I'll never be fit to command the Methden Garrison, but I don't care right now. And I don't think it was so horrible the rats found out. They can't take any advantage of us. They've not been in any action for over a month."

I let him go to sulk on his own. I knew his mood wouldn't last long. Instead, I turned my attention to filling my days until that birdwit decided to return. I refused to dread this inevitable occurrence, but I certainly didn't much look forward to it. Which meant I had to keep busy.

I resumed my quest in the library. I didn't find much beyond encounters and speculations. There was mention here and there of Detlev, the former Norsundrian commander. which I read with interest. Not too much information appeared about him. He hadn't been around our kingdom much—there had been magic spells laid to keep him out of the royal city—except when he appeared briefly at the end of the Regency. My guts lurched when I read that he confronted the king up above the Aladas Pass, the day the evil Regent vanished at last. That place would ever have a bad name, ever and ever; now each time I saw the word, I heard an echo of the high weird voices of the elders singing the Andahi Lament.

Anyway, I found out little, but it occupied my time. I also redoubled my efforts with the heavy cavalry broadsword one of us had stolen from the garrison that first crazy day before they got to the armory. I exercised with it until my arms and stomach ached.

Then, two days later, Tdor came to see me. And I knew the moment I saw her there'd been trouble.

"What happened?" I said as she sank down onto my bed with a sigh.

"I'm dusted. They finally let the fruit wagons through this morning. Had to search every basket, box, and barrel! We have been busy all morning. In fact I should be out now but my cart's empty, so I thought I'd stop by. That horrible

Norgiem came yesterday. They beat up dad, and two others of the men on our street, and said if we cause trouble we'll have our shipments stopped. And that rat's butt Norgiem watched with a little grin, like he was enjoying every kick and punch."

Norgiem was definitely the nastiest Norsundrian commander we'd had yet, and he obeyed that birdwit Llyenthur. I had to think about that, I resolved, as Tdor went on, "You know, nearly everyone in the city would starve if they stopped food-trade. All that's left are odd little gardens some have, and are those safe?"

"You know what they're doing, they're muzzling us without letting us fight."

She agreed, looking grim. "My da still hasn't said a word to us. He still wants to fight, and last night he got drunk earlier than ever. Not that anyone blames him, the way he looks. But Mother had us come in and told us we either have to quit running with you or run away. That's run away as far as the Norsundrians are concerned. She'd help us out when she could, but it'd have to be secret. Which means we'd have to find a place to stay."

"And?"

"We're talking it over. I guess we have until our next plan of action. I'd better go, I guess. How is it here?"

"Dull," I said. "Working out. Reading. Staying away from my family to avoid tiresome questions."

She grinned. "Well, I'm off. *All* the inns want fruit!" And she was soon gone.

That left me mostly alone. I shunned contact with my mother and sister. I couldn't bear the thought of being hailed before Imry Llyenthur in my mother-clothes, and I sensed that if he sent for me he wouldn't wait around while I changed. And Retren didn't come by. At first I thought he didn't because he knew no plan could be in the offing, but I discovered he was merely holing up in his room, sleeping and stuffing himself with food, but at least he was coughing less. I didn't hear that wark wark noise echoing from his room down the hall anymore.

Being mostly alone afforded me plenty of brooding time. The first interview seemed unreal, and also, the lack of conventional threats made the *potential* threat very great. I don't know why that was so.

But the summons came one afternoon. I'd fallen asleep over a book on siege tactics. The Norsundrian runner knocked on my door this time. I said, "Yeah?"

He opened the door. "Come with me."

Now that the summons was finally here, the whole thing seemed so much less horrible to me than the anticipation beforehand. I threw aside the book and followed. I was rested, dressed for action, and had my boots on. So the boots were a vanity. There was no way anyone could call them cavalry boots (though I had the toes squared like the dashing cavalry officers were doing) because cavalry heels were never over three fingers high—just enough to catch behind the stirrup—and mine were a little over that. These were town boots, and I know every warrior thinks town boots are foppish, which is why I wore my pants long and outside, but the extra fingers those boots added to my height—I thought my stature—gave me a hand-span of confidence.

Still, any inclination I might have felt to smile in triumph was killed when we went to my father's office again.

The flunky left me. The windows were both open, and pale sunlight flooded into the room.

"Good afternoon, Marend."

"Yeah, yeah. Uh, what do I call you?"

"I suppose my name will suffice." He looked very amused. "I answer to either one or both."

I shrugged. "That's right. You don't like titles, and I guess using insults wouldn't be acceptable."

"Would you feel insults give you a necessary advantage?"

"Only if it makes you mad."

He grinned. It was that sharing-the-joke one, and I fought not to grin back. I said, "It seems weird to me you haven't done anything to anybody here in Methden. I did some reading, and sure enough, it wasn't all rumor about Norsunder's history of conquering. Assassination. Nasty reprisals. Unless the writers of records lied. I don't think my Da would've kept any records full of lies. He said he went through 'em all about twenty years ago, after his visit to the king, and weeded out the wrong ones."

"History is written by the victors, surely you've heard

that mossy truism. It also depends on point of view. 'Norsunder' has a variety of goals, same as you find anywhere else. Just as policies vary from country to country, commanders vary in both goal and method of achieving those goals. As for savage reprisals, though they are popular with the warriors, they don't always produce the desired results. Marloven Hess is an excellent example. While Norgiem is quite fond of executions and the like, Methden's character is too much like its late jarl: I suspect the last person standing in this city — this kingdom — would be plotting even as we shot them."

"Then you did axe people in other countries?"

"Selectively, after the initial fighting. In Sartor, for instance, Bostian made specific promises as soon as he was in control. When the expected resistance took place, Bostian carried out our promises promptly and enthusiastically, and you should have seen how losing a few lives caused those patriotic lighters to suddenly reevaluate their priorities! All the high and sacred principles they mouth out so tediously just mean they put their own comfort above anything. The poorest houses in Sartor are tricked up much like the jarlan's suite here." He flicked his fingers toward the western wing.

And there was the usual twinge of disgust at this casual dismissal of Mother's parlor. His antipathy fitted my own sentiments! I protested, "But *Sartor*? We hear so much about it."

"Lighters like to propagate symbols and myths. Not that I underestimate the power of symbols. We use them very effectively ourselves." He smiled pleasantly, but his green eyes reminded me of stones. Bright, cold, and glittery. "Sartor's 'greatness' is one of their favorites. Sartor fell quickest of all. If you'd like to see the reports, I can show them to you. Later, perhaps, if time-pressure eases, I will take you there."

"Why are you doing all this stuff with me?"

He looked surprised. "Surely you do not indulge in false modesty, Marend? Heir to Jarl Jarend of Methden. Leader of a well-trained gang of underground resistance fighters. An asset of primary value in this country, don't you see?" He grinned. "And I have a specific post in mind for you."

"I'm not going to switch sides."

He sighed, affecting disappointment.

"What is your experiment?" I asked, then I added with sarcasm, "My brother thinks asking is tantamount to betrayal, so I just want to tell you, in case you agree with him."

"Another reason why I am interested in you, and not in your brother," he said gently, "is his—ah, caution."

I caught myself just as I was feeling I had triumphed. Backhanded! I'd have to watch myself!

"I'll do better; I'll take you to see them, but not now. I must leave soon. However, I brought you a couple of our military histories if you'd like to read something that I consider reasonably written." He picked up two books and held them out to me. "You can tell me what you think next time I come, and we can argue over their merits or shortcomings."

I opened one and saw an unfamiliar script. "Can't read it."

"I'll give you the language."

"I don't want to talk like Norsundrians."

His brows went up. "Marend! Are you afraid of a language?"

"Of course not!" I scoffed.

"Then why the reticence? It's a very useful language. Precise. Unsentimental."

I frowned. "You do it by magic?"

"Partially. Are you afraid I'll muddle with your mind?"

"Yes."

"That's rumor. If it was easy, do you think we would have gone to so much effort?" He flung his hand out in a gesture to include the city. Maybe the entire kingdom. "I'm simply going to give you knowledge of our language."

"And what else? I don't want any loyalty spell!"

He sighed, tipping his head as he regarded me. "What did I *just* say? I don't know who started that myth. Think, Marend. If loyalty spells worked, your father would be sitting here handing out my commands, saving me a great deal of effort."

I flushed at the mention of my father, then snarled, to hide it, "Some of you would be killing everybody anyway, for the fun of it. Like that Norgiem. Likes blood."

Llyenthur gave a crack of laughter. "You're right. He does. My point remains, there is no loyalty spell. There are spells that can distort or effect other aspects of the mental realm that—ah, can do significant damage, let us say, but it takes more effort than you might assume, and even difficult spells can be broken. But I promise. The spell I use is old, and simpler than the Universal Language Spell. It will just give you the one language."

If he tried something more, would I be able to fight it off? That thought smacked of cowardice. I shrugged. "All right." I thought to myself: he's making spying a lot easier, too. That banished all my doubts. "Go ahead." Birdwit!

He put his fingertips on my forehead as he murmured something, then there was a moment—less than half a breath—of a weird and unpleasant sort of expansion (in a mental way) then dizziness and a thread of headache-type pain behind my eyes. It lingered for a bit after he lifted his hand, then faded.

"I'll be back in a few days," he said in their language. I heard the sounds, the sense coming as a very fast echo. "You can tell me what you think." Pointing to the two books.

"Unless they put me to sleep," I said. And I left.

As I walked back, I thought about the conversation. There did not seem to me to be any advantage gained by either side—except I'd allowed Imry to give me that Norsundrian language. I wondered if it might not be a good idea for me to ignore his books, just in case he was feeling smug about my cooperation. "*Yes!*" I thought. "It's up to *me* whether I read 'em or not! If they were trying to force me to turn against my own country I wouldn't have the choice."

I ran down the stairs to my room.

Seven

IN THE HALLWAY, A shaft of light from somewhere flashed into a mirror, causing me to turn my head. I saw myself — yecch! Time and more to cut my hair! I scratched my neck, and felt a black curl lying right on my collar. Funny, how it creeps up on one.

I'd always got it cut at the garrison before. I had to seek a barber, which was an annoyance. I'd just come back from my haircut and was trying to decide whether to go to dinner or not (which meant mother-clothes) when Retren appeared at the top of the stairs.

"Wait!" he called, and he came galloping down. "Did you have to see that Imry Llyenthur? Sindan saw him, Norgiem, and a couple of the others on the river gate, looking south and jabbering. Sindan got close enough to realize they were blabbing in their language, so he left."

I was just about to tell him I knew it now, then I thought: why? He'll whine and nag about how I'm going to hop the fence to the other side. As if I would! Why not produce some results, *then* tell them?

"Yeah, briefly," I said. "The usual jawing. Told me Sartor fell quickest of all."

"You *believed* him?"

I shrugged. "Why would he lie about that? Said he'd show me the reports. Or take me there."

"*Take* you?"

"Yeah." I repeated Imry's statements about my importance, then I said, "But I told him I'm not going to join them."

Ret sighed. "I hate this. It'd be easier if they'd dump us in a dungeon," he muttered.

"They're fools!" I smirked. "Let's enjoy it!"

He jerked a scrawny shoulder up to his ear. "I guess. But this whole set-up makes me feel weird."

I opened my mouth to blast him, then I remembered how my feelings veered during my talks with Imry between thinking he was a real dolt and sensing I might be up against the post before my next breath. "It's the unexpectedness," I said to Retren. "The gang was prepared to fight them, and they didn't attack us. Then, just when we assumed we were going to get away with it, they come along and reveal they know who we are. Also, their leader isn't some giant, grizzled death's-head all dressed in black armor and armed with bloodstained weapons, like in the plays and ballads. Heh. Maybe his looking-like-anybody else image works for him in kingdoms where they've been lighters for centuries, and he doesn't see how *we'd* just think it stupid."

"You think that's it?" He looked relieved. "That *is* stupid."

I was glad to see Retren stop looking like a rabbit, but I knew almost as soon as the words were out it wasn't true. Well, not completely true. Maybe partly true? I remembered the books, and I thought, maybe I'll get some insight into the way they think from those. "I'll find out," I promised him.

We reached the dining room. I heard Mother's voice inside, addressing Lesra, and I paused. The thought of having to go back and change sparked and anger-fire in me. I supposed I'd have to skip dinner…but since the food was right there, waiting, it'd be efficient and convenient to eat it now.

The whole thing was so *pointless*, and worse, *hypocritical!*—

I thrust the door open with the heel of my hand and went to my place. Retren had already gone in, and as he passed Lesra's chair I saw his hand lift covertly and ruffle over Lesra's head. She looked up and grinned vacuously at him.

My mother turned her gaze my way; she checked, but said only, "Good evening, Marend."

I was braced for an argument; she gave the signal for us to be served. When I realized she was going to say nothing, my annoyance increased because I would not get the opportunity to have *my* say. So I said it anyway. "I am no longer willing to bow to another's hypocrisy."

"May we discuss it later?" Mother said gently.

I swept a hand scornfully. "Who are you afraid is going to overhear, Lesra or the servants? They *all* see me like this all the time; it's only *you* I've been forced into hypocrisy for."

"I'd prefer to wait," she said quietly, "because I'd like mealtimes to preserve a semblance of peace."

"More hypocrisy."

"If you call social pleasantries hypocrisy. I think of them as the superficial side of civilization," she murmured, "which make life much more comfortable. The rye rolls are on your right, Marend."

I looked up at the silent servant. "I don't want any."

He turned away.

I ate quickly. There was very little conversation, social pleasantry or otherwise. Though I'd won my point, I did not feel any particular triumph. My mother had not been defeated, or even convinced. She had merely withdrawn from the field of battle. I was victor only by default.

Which was a tactic, too.

Just, in fact, like—no. There was no comparison between my mother's cowardice and the Norsundrians' waiting. Yes, that's it. She was always weak, and cowardly, and they had the strength *when* they wanted it.

Hmm. I wonder if their book discusses strategy? My thoughts were broken when Retren rose, excused himself with an embarrassed mumble, and left. I got up and followed.

"Ret," I said in the hallway, "if you're going to be a sap, be honest about it. I detest phoniness more than I detest sentiment and mawkishness."

He shrugged, and blushed a little.

"I always thought you felt the same, unless you've lied to me, and what would be the point?"

"I *do* feel the same. But I like Les. You're wrong about her, you know. She's not at all stupid! I've been secretly teaching her a little about knife fighting. There's not much else to do, now't we're effectively grounded."

"Actually, that's a great idea. Just don't let Mother find out."

Retren flushed with pleasure, grinning. "I know. Les can keep a secret!"

We parted.

I had decided to begin reading, and I had to do it alone. On my way up, I thought about Lesra, and I realized what put me off about her most was her golden curls. Insipid, mawkish. Like my mother's.

I realized then that I hated my mother. I hated her stupid, weak, sentimental, weepy, cloying lack of Marloven determination. I'd hated it when she inspired Da's potential for the same, feelings that had come out as embarrassment when I was small. She and her golden hair hanging everywhere, and her velvet and lace — going on about the benefits of civilization in Telyerhas. Faugh! Why should I pretend I have any other feelings, because an accident of birth placed us in the same family? More hypocrisy!

Impatiently, I dismissed her from my mind, and I picked up those two slim, black-bound books. Apprehension pulsed within me when I opened the first, but it — both — turned out to be exactly what he'd said they were: military histories. Written by the commanders to illustrate strategies.

They were both from long ago, countries I didn't know, but I read them to learn something about Norsundrian thinking in strategy and tactics — their inside line of communication. They won the first war; the second book, I was surprised to find, illustrated a loss. The loss was by magic trickery, and a melodramatic attempt by a lighter to sacrifice himself (which did not come off) — but the writer felt this kind of tactic should be pointed out.

Eh, that's something, I thought.

And so I told Imry two days later, when he asked my opinion.

He laughed. "Did you expect we'd pretend we've never been defeated? Why? If we'd had nothing but successes, we'd've been in control years ago. Were you bored by them? Did they put you to sleep?"

"No. Read 'em both in one night."

"Then I'll give you a couple more. I'll give you one written by Detlev, outlining a new strategy that he developed about 150 years ago. You'll enjoy it, I think."

"Why'd he leave Norsunder?"

He shrugged. "I don't know, I haven't spoken to him for years. Probably figured he'd wield more power if he sided with the lighters, and he's right."

"I hadn't heard he'd taken over anywhere."

"Mm—just wait. He's one for biding his time. Of course, he may come back to us. He'll have forgotten how dull and weak most lighters are. Or, perhaps he's playing his own game. Who knows? We'll see."

He gave me more to read, and that was the pattern between us for about four weeks. He gave me books, I read 'em, and three or four days later we'd discuss them. We didn't talk about anything else during these short interviews. He gave me the impression he looked forward to taking time off from a very busy schedule for these visits.

I told him exactly what I thought, and what I would have done, after reading Detlev's report, which was about the disaster caused by an Norsundrian named Dzydes, back when my father was small. This idiot had control of Bereth Ferian, apparently an important place, though I had no idea where it was except somewhere north, but he let emotion blur his judgment, which was not very good anyway. Imry professed himself surprised at how quickly I mastered various details, and how much I was picking up about the art of command. He couldn't help wondering what I'd do with some real training!

"Too bad I won't switch sides." I smirked.

"I know. You don't see me offering the training, do you?" he retorted with that sharing-the-joke grin.

We got along pretty well. He was as sparing of compliments as my father had been, so I couldn't help taking them to heart—though of course I reminded myself they were just from a Norsundrian.

Meanwhile, the group was trying to come up with a plan.

Retren said when we had a midnight meeting in the

library that first week, "We've *got* to do something. I hate this sitting around."

There was general agreement, then Tdor said, "We'll all have to move first. Otherwise, what's to prevent them, since they know who we are, from coming in after the action's over, and smearing us?"

"We need to plan *well*," I said. "I'm learning a little about their strategy. If we wait a bit, I can learn enough to turn against them with some effect."

"Don't go too far with it," Tdor said, shaking her head.

"Why the sudden fear? Imry Llyenthur promised there is no such thing as a loyalty spell, I don't know anything about magic, so I can't prove it's true, but we've never heard a lot of orders concerning such things have we? Just rumors and guesses? And for the rest, I see nothing wrong with exploring the unknown as long as my will is intact, and my will is stronger than *theirs*!"

The others were silent, and Tdor said with a shade less conviction, "Walk soft, Marend. Walk soft and keep your sword loose."

Eight

ALMOST TWO WEEKS SLID by then. I didn't notice them much because I was absorbed in my reading, and in rethinking plans for how to turn around losses in case Imry Llyenthur asked what I would have done—a question I thoroughly enjoyed.

Then one night, Retren came unexpectedly to my room while I was reading. He'd been around seldom of late so I was surprised when my door opened and he walked in. I shut the book more quickly than I would have done to any other type of book—and his eyes caught the movement.

"Marend, the gang wants to plan something," he started. "They're beginning to feel this wait is just a clever defeat..." His voice trailed off as his took in the books on the bed.

The bindings were all a plain, utilitarian black but the titles were listed in easily readable lettering on spine and front. Norsundrian lettering.

His eyes flashed wide, then narrowed, just like Mother's.

"Before you start whining," I said corrosively, "let me tell you I've had their language and I've been reading these military histories for almost a month, with no ill effects. All they are's reports! Right now I'm comparing their version of a mission in one of the old Venn colonies and a version Da had sitting on the shelves, moldering away. Know what? There's not much difference. Except the Norsundrian one seems to be better organized and more concise."

"The writers were probably flogged to death otherwise," he retorted sarcastically. "Why are you *defending* that stuff?"

"I just told you. I don't want to listen to you nagging about whether I'm hopping the fence or not, so I'm forestalling your accusations that I'm avidly reading secret indoctrination material by telling you what and why I'm doing it. Believe me, I'm learning lots. And when I get enough, I intend to turn my knowledge back on them, and *smash* them!"

"How do you get these books?"

"Imry gives 'em to me."

"I thought we'd agreed they didn't deserve names."

I sighed. "See how far that pointless game got us?"

He picked up a book reluctantly, turned it over, then said slowly, "You read 'em and talk about 'em and he tells you more stories about the stuff in 'em, is that it?"

"That's all. And very illuminating I find it, a firsthand look at how they think."

"Marend." His eyes were round with horror. "That's just what you used to do with Da." Then his face changed, and my anger at his words exploded into action.

I got up and across the room in a second, and I pinned him against a wall. "And so you're going to run off and whine to the others I'm finding a new father, huh? How could you be so stupid? This is *nothing* like lessons with Da, *nothing!* Understand?"

He pressed his lips together, then shoved my hands away from his shoulders.

"I'll warn you once," I said in my deadliest voice. "Though we're nearly eye to eye I can—*easily!*—wipe up the floor with you. Don't cross me."

He pushed past me and left.

The next day, I had another meeting with Llyenthur, and got some more books. At first, very much despite myself, I was edgy, that comment of Retren's still writhing away in my stomach-pit, but Imry made me laugh by a droll account of his trying to toughen up a weak and wobbling idiot who was part of his early training. It sounded like he was stuck with a herd of buffoons, fools, and clod-hoppers during his boyhood years. Then he went into how dealing with buffoons made it so much easier to trip up buffoons who thought they were his superior in the days when he was not a lot older than I.

Did *they* learn the hard way!

As I laughed, I thought, what a fool Retren is! Here's this blabbermouth sitting on the edge of the desk, telling stories about former inferiors, and superiors. He couldn't be more unlike Da, who was always respectful toward the king and to the stable hands and carters alike. And who always sat straight and tall behind his desk, neatly dressed and imposing in his uniform or his House tunic in a non-military formal occasion, his hair cut and his boots shined. A proper symbol of command!

I was just as glad Retren stayed out of my way. He could sulk all he wanted. He'd better stay out of my sight or I *would* wipe up the floor with him.

An agreeable addition that I wasted no time on probing the reason for was the complete cessation of summonses from my mother. I consequently saw nothing of her or Lesra, and that pleased me.

If only I had the freedom to leave the castle, everything would be perfect.

Then Tdor came to see me. It was a Fifthday morning. She climbed up to the library and came in the old way. I was working out with the broadsword.

She grinned. "Itching to get out?"

"Aren't I just," I said, putting my sword down.

She rubbed her hands. "I can imagine. How I'd hate to be grounded! Particularly now that it's warming up a little!"

"What's going forward?"

She shrugged. "We want to make a plan. And I wanted to come, and see for myself what you're doing, reading Norsundrian books."

Anger twisted inside me.

"Now, don't start in on me." She waved a hand. "I wanted to see for myself. I know you forbade Retren to tell us, but that's between you two."

I mastered my temper, and told her what I'd been reading and why. She listened without interruption, and looked curiously at a couple of the books, then tossed them on the bed.

At the end, she grunted, then gave another of her abrupt one-shoulder shrugs. "Inside line of communication, huh? Well, if you say it's all right. But you know, I've got a creepy feeling about the whole thing."

I sighed.

"I know, I know, it sounds rabbity, and all that, but that's *still* what I think. And one thing I do trust is my instincts, same's Ma. Maybe it'd be better if you reported in to us, the way you used to."

"I will if all the nagging ceases. What about this wish for a plan? Do you want to call a meeting here?"

"Yeah," she said, looking at me straightly, "if *everyone* can come."

"Everyone?" I repeated, fire boiling inside me.

"Yep. Fact is, the rats want to do something, too. Called a general meeting couple weeks ago. We've had three now, actually, and y'know, they're a pretty good bunch—"

"No wonder Ret's not dared to face me! But I never thought that coward would be traitor enough to go behind my back—"

"Coward! Traitor! Behind your back," she scoffed. "C'mon, Marend, listen to yourself. You *know* things change! Ramond isn't so bad. Squirrely about art, maybe, though I have to admit nobody draws a horse the way he does. And he took all the blame for the original fight onto himself, and pointed out, very reasonably, I thought, that with the Norsundrians here it's just *stupid* to feud forever. Very handsome, I thought it, for him to concede we were much better than his gr—"

"So that was his plan all along," I said. I was so angry my teeth ground together. "My salute to him, but that you were *stupid* enough to believe his—"

"What's stupid about an apology? Look, Marend, you did us a lot of good, starting the group, taking in only those of us who'd never be accepted as recruits. Even the ones who died got respect from others, from *themselves*, and their memories are as well-thought-of as the warriors! And thanks to you it's been two years since Sindan even thought of his bad eye, and Rom's now hot with a bow and doesn't care about his leg, and so on! But when you act like this I begin to think Retren's right, and you don't really care about us at all, at least not anymore — all you care about is being in command!"

"I'm in command because I'm best fitted to be," I said.

"So," she flung up her hands, "prove it! Meet with Ramond."

"Prove it! I've been proving it for years!" I shouted. "And you cowardly rabbits have gone—"

"Oh, stop with the coward talk. Nobody is a coward. I'll come back when you've cooled off."

I was so close to closing my fingers around her neck I had to stand still until she'd left. Then I picked up my knife and threw it, and watched it thud to the hilt in the door right where her head had been.

"Why are you so angry?" Imry asked three days later, when I went up to see him.

"Backstabbing. Never mind," I said shortly.

"Your group has changed loyalties now that you're racked up?"

Anything less than honesty would be contemptible. Particularly, I thought, when he seems to know the answer as well as I — probably better. "If I'd had better control, it wouldn't be happening," I said bitterly, hating the words.

"Your brother the spearhead, I trust?" He put his head to one side.

The anger flowered again, bright and hard and painful, at my impotence.

He smiled. "My compliments to Retren." He flicked up a hand. "I hadn't thought him that clever."

Neither had I. I'd seen him as a follower, and a weak one at that, for so long, it didn't occur to me until then that he'd shifted his allegiance around me. Maybe he even wanted to command, the way Da always intended, no matter how hard I tried. I clenched my teeth hard on a retort.

Imry Llyenthur said mildly, "He and his new friends plan to resume their efforts against us? Who are these new friends? Additions beside the greengrocer twins, the boy with the bad knee..." He named my entire gang.

I was so angry that I thought to myself, if he could teach me their spying skills I'd get a gray jacket made that very day.

"Never mind," I said. "They're birdwits. And I strongly suspect, come to think of it, they'll just talk a lot and nothing'll come of it."

"That's what I thought," he said, smiling faintly.

Two nights later they proved me wrong.

The following morning Llyenthur sent for me. As soon as I saw him, that weird danger-sense flowed around me. Nothing was different. He was perched on the edge of the side-table reading something when I came in. And he looked like usual — no weapons in sight, overlong and unkempt hair parted in the middle and straying down, a baggy tunic with no shirt underneath, light brown long trousers, and mocs. Where was the danger?

He dropped the paper. "The animals seem to be restless in the springtime," he commented, as if continuing a conversation.

"What?" I blinked.

"Last night your erstwhile friends ambushed the night patrols at the shift-change point."

Only astonishment kept me from laughing.

"That is, they attempted to do so. I'd thought it best to be prepared just in case."

"That's *my* plan—" I bit off that yelp of outrage, and forced out a question in a more normal voice, "What happened?" Though it came out sounding kind of strangled.

"Casualties, you mean?"

"Yeah."

"We have six in the infirmary, four of 'em serious. I don't know your numbers. We saw two bodies before they Disappeared." He frowned in concentration. "A towhead who apparently had a hearing problem—"

"Kovar," I whispered. "Somebody forgot his signals..."

"The engagement was short, but very active. The other was a brawny youth, red hair—"

I shrugged. "A rat. Not one of mine."

"I don't know how many wounded. Quite a number is my guess. They scarpered in all directions when I gave the signal to disengage. I was unable to spot a leader as he was completely unable to rally them."

I shook my head. "*Bird*wits."

"Agreed." He still smiled but it wasn't the joke one. It didn't reach his eyes. "I'm inclined to make an example. Ah! I forgot to mention we took three prisoners. I really desire an end to the strife! What do you think I should do?"

"Who are they?"

"None of them would give their names, though of course I know who your brother is. If you were in my position, what would be your course of action?"

"Retren—" I said, and smacked the table—then yelped, "Shit!"

"Is that a judgment or a suggestion?" He laughed.

I struggled to fight the anger down. To control it. Make it serve me, instead of it taking over. I said with a pretty fair assumption of calm, though I could feel my heart tick-ticking in my forehead, "What are you going to do? Kill 'em?"

"Ah, I thought I would discuss this with you. I regard this as an excellent opportunity to test your skills as a leader. You grasp theory very well, but in practice?" His brows went up. "I'd had it in mind to send you to a training camp I'm setting up further north, but in many respects I'm impressed enough with you to think you might do better right here. If you were to successfully handle—say—this situation I'd pull Norgiem out and give you command of this city."

"Command?" I repeated, stunned.

"Your standing order would be, simply, to maintain peace."

"*I'd* be in charge?"

"You'd only be answerable to me. You would be Commander Ndarga, which would require you to move to the garrison command wing," he added.

"But—as a Norsundrian?"

"I thought by now you'd see the old sentiments against us as the hypocrisy they are. Unless you're worried about what people would think of you? You've already seen how you and I agree in most essentials. You know I wish merely to establish in this country the most effective and efficient organization possible."

"But why—why all this?" I managed.

"Mmm. I will enter into my motives, and intentions when you have demonstrated yourself worthy of my confidence. I have very few close associates! There is no necessity to answer me at once, you know. Go think it over. I'll be here off and on, ah, for most of the next couple days."

"What about Retren and the others?"

"They can languish in the garrison lockup." He flicked his fingers toward the window. "A couple days' sitting behind bars might be beneficial. It will certainly free up people who are better employed rebuilding, now that spring appears to be here at last."

I walked out slowly, my mind so jammed with different thoughts I hardly knew where I was going. Retren's perfidy, stupidity, and predicament warred in my brain. Impossible to focus, when my thoughts were constantly splintered by: Tdor's visit; the rats' taking over my group; Imry's invitation; even Da's death. What would he think of me? If he was a ghost, what exactly would he see? He's always said that Ret must do well at the academy, and once he did, he would be the heir. I was to help train him for that. And this would have been the spring when he would go to the royal city to start.

All these thoughts gnawed at me inside. All my life I'd been taught—by Da!—that Norsunder was the enemy. It was a simple fact of life. They were evil, they intended to take Marloven Hess—that much was true!—and force our army to fight to their commands. But so far in my experience, only one of those things was true, the invasion. And invading was scarcely confined to Norsunder.

"Evil." What really was evil? So far, Imry Llyenthur seemed to be a blabbermouth, but otherwise easygoing. Unsentimental, which I liked. Scornful of lighter hypocrisy, which I also liked, especially the mushy hypocrisy of courts and fuss and flounces. Evil was going around slaughtering everyone in sight, wasn't it? But that's what happens in battle. Are both sides evil, then?

No. We are not.

We. Who exactly was this *we*, right now? That brought me squarely up against the betrayal of my group, and the results, three of which were waiting in the garrison lockup.

I reached no conclusion, and so I tried to distract myself by reading, but I had trouble doing that. I couldn't eat, I couldn't even take a walk on the high wall above the river. I was completely alone that day. And despite my strongest efforts of will, my mind would not clear.

At night, it was worse. I finally left my rumpled bed on which I'd been tossing sleeplessly and roamed the halls, stopping every so often to stare down through the windows at the dark-wrapped garrison.

Dawn had just barely grayed, revealing a rainy day, when there was a knock at my door, and my mother walked in. Her eyes were red and puffy, but her expression was surprisingly remote.

"Marend, will you ask your friend to free your brother?"

"Friend? You mean Imry Llyenthur?"

"Yes."

"He's *not* my friend —"

She interrupted. "Will you, or won't you?"

"I can't. I mean I can, but it would be a waste of time."

"Then I will," she said, and she left.

I sighed. What good could *she* possibly do? But her face, hopeless and cold, stayed with me.

I went down to the kitchen to get some coffee. It did not clear my head much. I finally decided to go up to the tower.

Imry Llyenthur was there, with a couple other Norsundrians. When I walked in he looked at them, and they vanished — by magic. Disconcerting.

He said wryly, "I just sustained a visit from your esteemed mother."

"Esteemed," I muttered, the coffee boiling inside me. "She collared me this morning."

He sighed. "I felt I was — unwillingly — taking part in a very bad play. 'Take me and free my son.' Now, what possible use would she be? And if I'd found a use, I would have implemented it long ago. I did try to explain these things to her, but she was so busily emoting I've a notion I was merely wasting time for both of us."

A vague, unsettling sense of shame made me even more nauseated. I could not tell if it was on behalf of my mother or because of her. Her decision to confront Imry Llyenthur was certainly no fault of *mine*. "She's a fool," I said loudly and forcefully, which seemed to burn off the shame. "Don't pay any attention to her."

"I hadn't intended to." He smiled. "Tell me! What do you recommend we do in our present situation?"

"I thought of one thing," I said hesitantly. My mother's performance swam up in my mind again, robbing my words of conviction. "Maybe Ret and the others'll promise not to cause any more problems."

His eyelids lifted in exaggerated surprise. "Surely there isn't a little of your mother in you?"

"Of course not," I scoffed. "It's the neatest solution. Takes the least amount of effort on anyone's part."

"Shall we go ask him?"

I hesitated. At first I thought, *he* shouldn't go with me. Then I thought, well, it doesn't matter if Imry hears or not because if they promise, we can't exactly keep it secret!

"Let's go." I shrugged.

He walked beside me to the main stairway, down that, through the hall leading to the courtyard, and out. I saw no one, but I felt that eyes were on us, and pride made me keep my head up and back straight. Whatever happened was *my* decision, I reminded myself, and this gave me a little infusion of confidence.

It was still raining outside. I realized it was the first time I'd set foot out-of-doors for all this time.

We entered the garrison. The familiar sights and smells hit me—the Norsundrians hadn't changed it much at all. The warriors halted in their tasks to salute Llyenthur, not a hand to the chest like us, but hand raised, palm out, like, *I have no weapon in hand*. He ignored most, but smiled once or twice. The ones who seemed to come and go freely in his presence appeared to be some sort of special staff.

No one was in the lock-up, except for a couple guards and the three. Two of them were rats, as I'd thought. And there, looking skinny and small and rumpled, was Retren. He was sitting on a bunk staring up at a window. At the sound of our footsteps on the stone floor his head turned. He had a purple eye, and a scabbed-over cut on his jaw. When he saw me, his expression hardened from pensive and tired to cold and remote. I saw a strong resemblance in his face to our mother.

"I want to ask you something, Retren," I said. I would have liked to say more, but I felt constrained by the rats' and Llyenthur's presence to be direct.

Ret got up from the bunk and came a little way toward the door. "The *one* good thing," he started clearly, "about being in here, I'd thought, was I wouldn't have to talk to *you*, Marend." His voice quavered on my name.

Did he realize his words were a death-sentence? I said in a rush, "You can come out if you'll promise to keep the peace."

Those last three words slipped in when I couldn't bring myself to say *stop fighting against them*. Weren't we supposed to be fighting against Norsunder?

I wavered right there, fighting a fierce inner debate as my brother and I locked gazes, with the bars between us.

"Peace. That's what you call it now?" one of the rats asked, voice thin with scorn that didn't quite hide all the fear.

This entire interview is absurd, I thought, but my gut churned, my skin itched, and I had just enough awareness to think *I wish it was just absurd*.

Then Retren gave me a look of inexpressible scorn, and returned to his bunk.

"Retren," Llyenthur spoke suddenly, pleasantly, over my head. "Your mother has requested permission to visit you. Shall I send her down here?"

"Yes," Retren said clearly, looking straight at me. "Please."

In surprise I turned to Llyenthur. He gave me the wry sharing-the-joke grin, like we were allies against Ret and my mother. I gave him a shrug (as much to show Retren well, who cares about *you* then, as anything else) and we left.

That door is closed, I told myself firmly, but an echo of that horrible sorrow I'd felt at Da's death burned at the corners of my eyes, and burrowed under my ribs.

I tightened my gut, reaching for the steadying anger, reminding myself that I must control it, and not let it control me

When Llyenthur said, "So, Marend?" I braced myself and stated with a reasonably copy of his own lightness and indifference, "Time for an alternative, of course."

"I'll leave that to you. I've urgent business elsewhere, right now, and a number of people clamoring for my attention. Why don't you come up here tonight? I'd like to take you on a little trip."

"All right," I said, squashing down anticipation.

Nevertheless, I felt it. All day, while the anguish of Retren's scorn echoed again and again in my mind, I sought relief by wondering what kind of trip?

Surely, by magic! And because everything else was so grim I forced myself to be honest about the fact that I was proud Imry Llyenthur had singled me out from all the other people in Methden, and thought me qualified for a command position. He didn't even know Ramond's *name!* And once I realized I'd been honest—unhypocritical— relief was followed swiftly by enjoyment. Why not? What was wrong with being the best? I'd trained hard all my life to be the best!

I thought about being the best, and about command, and about Imry's organization based on efficiency and skill. Not on "honor" and "loyalty" and other words that the weak used to control the strong. I thought about those things so that I did not have to think about Retren in the prison, under death sentence.

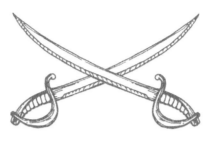

Nine

My ANTICIPATION INCREASED AS the day ended.

I couldn't stomach the prospect of eating, so I decided this was an excellent opportunity to practice strength of will, and I went up to the tower at sundown.

No one was there. I lit a lamp, looked around, and discovered that I had come to regard the room more as Imry's than as Da's. Moreover, these last few visits had ended with more praise than scolding, unlike my trips to the tower to face my father. The fear was gone—fear of disappointing him, fear of being a disappointment no matter how mightily I strove to be bigger, stronger, better than I was. It had never been good enough.

Except now it *was* good enough. *I* was good enough.

Command! The thing I had believed forever denied me!

I sat down to wait, but that soon made me restless. I got up and idly poked around, looking for something to do. Not nosing—not spying, I thought defensively, then I realized, that's how I'd think about an ally's stuff, not an enemy's.

An ally. Ah—be honest, you abhor hypocrisy, I told myself. You want to be Imry Llyenthur's ally—if he didn't call himself a Norsundrian, you'd've done it a week or two ago.

What was it I'd thought, when realizing my true feelings about my mother? But for accident of birth. Why should I give a spit about what my family thinks, when really, blood-relation is just another of those lighter sentiments? How many families stay together because of that, and really detest each other? Marloven history is full of brother killings—the former king had died by his brother's hand. The only one I really felt kinship had turned on me.

Retren—

Blood-relation clearly meant nothing to *him* anymore.

There was nothing of interest in that room in any case: reports, mostly local, and several lists of things I did not recognize. I picked up the lamp, walked out, and opened the bedroom door. I'd thought I never would, then reminded myself that freedom from sentiment was strength.

I held the lamp high. The plain room was utterly untouched. I could tell no feet but mine had stepped in for half a year. It was painfully tidy, yet still there was a lingering aura of Da's personality, even though he'd only slept there occasionally, when work or weather kept him there late.

I closed the door again.

When I got back to the office I sensed a charge in the air, a little like the way it feels after a bolt of lightning strikes close. Magic? I didn't know; I had no experience of it. I knew it was not yet midnight. I hadn't closed my eyes for a day and a half, and my lids were a little gritty, but I was wide awake. Strong-willed, that's me.

The air flickered, and Imry Llyenthur appeared in the doorway. He was wearing the black and gray of a Norsundrian, which was unpleasantly startling in effect.

"Ah, sometimes—tiresome necessity—the trappings are useful. Remember what I said about symbols?" he greeted me, smiling.

I assented with a gesture so I wouldn't have to speak, then looked down myself in my old black night-sneak clothes. Military-plain, as unlike my mother's soft and foppish "civilization" as possible. Practical. Not to mention (if I was honest) it made me look taller, and it hid the dirt.

"You've been one of us all along," he said gently. "Can you admit it now?"

"Why not?' I said, shrugging. "Let's go!"

He took me to a number of places. I saw ancient Eidervaen, which was a mess. I was much more impressed with the big grim Chwahir fortress in the Land of the Chwahirs' capital Narad, where a fierce-eyed old man in a black robe deferred to Llyenthur and obviously hated it. The atmosphere there made me shudder, but for an example of dominance in physical form, I'd never seen anything more effective

We went to half-a-dozen cities — and each transfer hurt a bit more than the previous, but I kept my jaw clenched. If he didn't complain, I wouldn't.

I saw huge and excellently organized military camps, border emplacements, etc. Everywhere, I witnessed respect, hatred, and fear in faces when Llyenthur appeared, but always they — whether Norsundrian or lighter, prisoner or free — consciously or unconsciously waited for him to speak, to comment, to order. What I saw, and was intoxicated and exalted by, was the effect of virtually unlimited power. I had craved just this, all my life. I had worked for it as hard as I could.

I looked about me and I thought, command of Methden's garrison was only a beginning. There would be no quarter for weakness — in myself, in others — until I too had reached the desired heights.

Imry said almost nothing to me, and did not introduce me to anyone until the next to last place.

This was a palace. I have no idea where. Even someone as uninterested and unknowledgeable as I am about "art" could see the harmony in the lines of its architecture.

We appeared in a large room that overlooked a spring-bare garden (it was daytime here so I knew we were halfway round the world). Two men were there, one tall, dark-haired man with a little beard that accentuated the sharp bones of his face. He was sitting, reading a book. The other stood by the window, his face profiled, his long hair so white it was nearly blue, and so fine it drifted almost like smoke. He showed no expression, and never so much as glanced at us. He was beautiful, but like winter ice.

The atmosphere shimmered with that lightning-bolt charge of magic, and even in my exalted mood danger curled warningly in my stomach, though no one moved or said anything.

Llyenthur said aloud only, "This is Marend Ndarga," to the bearded one, and to me, "And this is Svirle of Yssel."

I had never heard of Yssel.

This Svirle looked my way. Instinctively I dropped my gaze, but still there was an instant's mental pain. My mind blanked—was not my own for a heartbeat, and I gasped, and then was myself again, as he turned away with an obvious lack of interest, saying something dismissive in another language.

Llyenthur laughed, said, "But it'll work," in the Norsundrian language. Did he want me to understand?

We transferred, and appeared in a wide, high room that looked out over torchlit walls. It reminded me a little of our castle at home in details like the fortress-feel modified by wide windows and decorative materials hiding the basic stone of walls and floor. Other things, too, though I couldn't name what they were.

"We're in your capital now," Llyenthur said to me, as I leaned dizzily against the wall, my breathing shaky from reaction. He moved to the desk and glanced at an array of papers there. Then he slanted an inquiring glance my way. "No reaction?"

He did not mean reaction to the magic. I hid the physical effect, and as carelessly as I could, I said, "Huh. I was just thinking, it feels a little like home."

He smiled. "I felt that way myself when I first entered this castle." I must have showed my surprise because he said, "No, I'm not a countryman of yours, but my father was born here. In this castle, in fact." He looked around ruminatively. "He must've constructed my first home on the same general lines, which would explain the vaguely familiar feeling I'd had."

"This is the king's castle?"

"Yes. Why, are you impressed?" He laughed at me.

"My father's been here a lot," I said. "Do you know where the king is?"

"No." He grinned. "I wish I did!"

"My mother says he will return."

"Your mother is right," he said, his eyes reflecting the torchlight with dancing flames. He picked up a handful of papers, and raised his hand. "Back to Methden. There's work to be done."

We appeared in the tower office, and I flopped down and gulped for air. I think the only reason I wasn't puking and muttering the Waste Spell over and over was because there was nothing in my stomach to hurl.

"So what did you think?" He dropped his papers and sat down.

Locking my legs to steady them, I rose, then prowled around the room. When I could trust myself to speak normally, I told him pretty much what I wrote above.

"Which brings us back to Methden," he said. "Do you have a plan?"

I shrugged. "I don't know. Remember what you said about reprisals and executions and that? I don't see how a public execution is going to do anything but raise the entire city. Particularly Retren! My father was really popular, you know. That pretty much reflected on us."

"You forget your own position." He opened his hand toward the garrison. "And reputation. They all know you're tough. Uncompromising. I think, very possibly, if you are seen to be in command, Methden will calm down very quickly."

"A public execution?" Uncertainty hit me. I saw faces surrounding me —

"No. A public execution is either a demonstration of power to a weak populace, or a challenge to a restive one. It's enough to carry it out right here. Then it's merely the neatest and most effective way to rid yourself of trouble-makers. Word will get out anyway, and will serve as a warning to would-be dissidents. It's as well," his tone changed slightly, "that your insubordinate brother will make one of the number. The population will know you mean what you say, and that no one is exempt."

"You're right," I said, though the moment I said it, memories of Retren flickered, and my guts churned again. Little things — his holding my hand when he was small, his unwavering attention when I told him a story, his leaning against me and falling asleep. I knew if I brought them up I'd be laughed at for sentiment, for stupid things.

I must be strong. If I can't be strong, how can I comm- and an army renowned for its strength?

"Yes," I said firmly.

"Then I'll leave you to give orders as you see fit. I do have one request, though." He glanced down at the papers on his desk. "I want to be present when you carry it out."

Surprised, I said, "Don't you see executions all the time? Or..." I stiffened my spine, remembering that command was in my grasp. I had to be tough. "...is it you don't think I'll shoot my insubordinate brother?"

"Insubordinate brothers," he repeated, then laughed. "I'll need three watches or so," he said.

"Do you have to sleep?" I asked, suppressing the urge to rub my tired eyes. Oh, if they have a spell to avoid sleepless nights—!

"Occasionally. Unfortunately." As disappointment struck me he added, "Wait here. Norgiem will report to you." He disappeared.

Which is what happened. The slab-faced, hawk-nosed ex-commander presented himself and listened silently as, in Da's old manner, I outlined what was to occur the next day.

Once he was gone I sat down behind Da's desk, noticing that the papers Imry Llyenthur had brought had gone with him. I expected to feel that power, the triumph, the joy of replacing Da as I deserved, and had worked so hard for—but all I felt was a weird emptiness.

Tomorrow, I thought finally, as I got up. When I have accomplished something, I will feel it. And I'll be able to sleep again.

I started toward my room, then remembered Da's room. No one else was using it. Should I move there, to prove I was in command, and that sentiment no longer haunted me?

I went in, but Da's aura was still there, and though I struggled mightily to suppress sentiment, I could not get past the conviction that Da would be so disappointed that his will had not been carried out: that Retren wasn't in this room. There was no possibility of sleep. Finally I returned to my room, but sleep eluded me there as well. I roamed the empty corridors back to the office, sat down, and at last began to doze, but a nightmare shocked me awake. I left, and spent the rest of that endless night walking.

By dawn the nausea was back. I breathed hard to control it. Exhaustion strained my vision, making movement hurt. To fight it I returned to my room, and worked out until dizziness threatened to overcome me. Still, I kept at it. I was now fiercely awake, and by concentrating on performing each move perfectly, I remained in the immediate, which banished the hot tide of acid brought by unwanted memory.

The day passed in excruciating drips. The courtyard below the office — where executions had been held in the past — looked empty, but it did not feel empty. I had this sense that eyes gazed on it, and on my window, though I saw no one. Tension made my fingers jittery.

By tomorrow, everything will be done, and I will be in command.

A commander must be strong.

But first I had to get through today.

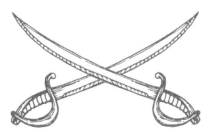

Ten

IMRY LLYENTHUR FINALLY APPEARED just as the sun was setting. I thought there was an edge of anger in the set of his mouth, and in his narrowed eyes. A last, horizontal beam of sunlight slanting in revealed marks of sleep-lessness beneath his eyes.

"Trouble?" I said.

"Not Detlev *again*," he muttered, as the sunbeam dissolved into shadow, and darkness closed in on the courtyard. "I wonder who's waving the old man's image at me this time," he added with such extreme dryness that I didn't know whether to laugh or hold my breath. "Never mind, Marend. A very clumsy attempt at distraction, which I'll have to address later. Carry on."

I went to the window and raised my hand in the signal—my first command.

A riding marched out of the prison, the three con-demned walking between their neat rows. All three had their hands tied behind them. I looked down at their faces, all three blanched and wretched in the torchlight.

Retren was marched to the wall. Torchlight shone on his upturned face as he gazed straight up at me. Nausea churned in my empty guts. I fought it, as Llyenthur came to stand next to me at the window.

The archers nocked arrows. Raised their bows. I closed my fist. And held my breath, willing it to be over.

A flicker caught at my vision from the rooftop. It *couldn't* be—

But before disbelief and nausea and the signal could make any headway with me an arrow flashed, an impossibly good shot, and thudded squarely in Norgiem's chest.

The guards jerked, snapping their faces toward the direction the shot had come in. No one was in sight. They looked skyward, to both sides, and when we did not see anyone, they all turned toward our window for orders.

Beside me Llyenthur said something under his breath, then raised a hand in his familiar magic gesture.

Nothing happened.

He sighed, not quite hiding the anger; his eyes were closed, which I did not understand at the time, but later I learned that he was handing out mental commands and searching on the mental plane.

That was when a swarm of figures flowed over the walls; both inner and outer perimeter sentries had been taken out in total stealth. In the space of three heartbeats they cut down the guards below, grabbed the prisoners, and one of the shrouded figures paused. It was a small one. A face turned up toward my tower window.

Tdor! She flipped up the back of her hand at me, and bolted after the rescue an instant before the roused garrison guards appeared from the other direction in pursuit.

Llyenthur had not moved. I could tell by his breathing that he was very angry, his gaze intent as he scanned the darkness from our vantage.

When the court was empty, I said, seeing my chance at command fleeing with that rescue party, "I recognize two of 'em. Let *me* run 'em down!"

"Go," Llyenthur said absently. Then he focused on me, as if it took an effort. "Take a riding with you. I suggest you dispatch them on the spot. Prisoners at this point will be a setback. Old loyalties die hard, I find; I shall," he said, teeth showing, "await my brother."

That surprised me. He'd mentioned a father but not a brother, except for that comment about insubordination, but I had taken that to be general—more of his tendency to blab. I didn't pause to question it. I ran downstairs to the garrison. The rest of the off-watch garrison guards were just assembling when I appeared. "A riding to follow me," I said.

They just stood there.

"Llyenthur says," I yelled, my voice cracking.

One looked at the others on the name Llyenthur, and then they moved fast.

I seethed with fury. The first thing I should do, I decided, was to have everyone flogged who didn't leap to my commands. If I had to use the words *Llyenthur says* one more time, they'd all die, and let's see who is in command.

They rode behind me in twos as I led the way through the silent streets; I hadn't slept in two days, so it didn't occur to me to question why I'd seen no servants, no people, even.

Though I'd seen Tdor, and knew that one of the other teen-sized figures had to have been Sindan, I led the Norsundrians straight to Ramond's.

As Llyenthur said, old loyalties die hard.

I barely noticed it was raining again. Rage was my fuel now, for I'd also not eaten for those two days. Rage, and a ferocious hunger for vengeance. The rats were *not* going to destroy my triumph. They'd die first, and they'd die witnessing my having won—

Ah, my thought processes ought to be familiar enough by now. We rode along the jumble of streets in the southern section of the city, well known to me. No one was about, and I was distracted by covert whispers between some of those riding behind me, a sign of disrespect. I tried to formulate a withering remark as we passed under the old bridge, when dark clad figures dropped down, startling the horses. More closed in from between the dark houses.

One figure rose from a roof, bow ready—another from the bridge—twang, twang!

The two Norsundrians flanking me fell, then the four behind them.

I leaped off my horse—no weapon! Snatching a long dagger from the side of a fallen Norsundrian, I discovered two pale faces closing in. Teens! I slashed at them with aim meant to kill, and as they faded back I dashed into a dark alleyway. But I knew that alley, and figured they had to have the other end blocked.

So I would go over the rooftops.

I scrambled up the stairs, having forgotten the one on the roof. I reached it just as a figure straightened up from behind a chimney to meet me.

All I could see was a silhouette: male, taller than me.

But everyone in the *world* was taller than me. I readied my knife as the warrior reached for me. I slashed. He feinted and blocked with an expert twist against my forearm, his strength driving my blade down and away. I turned with the block, meaning to whirl and use the momentum to lunge at him, but his foot hooked round my ankle and yanked.

I crashed onto the roof tiles. Pain flashed across my vision as my shoulder smashed onto the rough, broken edge of the ceramic rain-gutter. A skinny knee thumped my breath from my middle, and hands pinned my outflung arms wide. Rain and black spots ran in my eyes, I made no sense of what I saw.

"Got Marend," someone said breathlessly — a teen's voice.

"Let's go," another, older, low voice spoke.

Fingers dug into my arms, hauling me to my feet. I gritted my teeth as fire licked down my shoulder and arm. Then there was a short nightmare trip back down the stairs. I raged against defeat — dizziness — the smashing of my plans — as I looked about me desperately for any means of escape.

I recognized the trees planted along the street of fine merchants' houses; we ducked between two of the houses, through a service doorway, and I was pushed into a narrow vestibule with five or six people crowded into it. The door snapped shut behind us.

Among the faces circling me were Tdor and Rom and Harec. The rest were unknowns.

The crowd fell away. I found myself standing alone, facing a straight-shouldered young man, as rain-soaked as I was. He perched on the edge of a serving table in exactly the same manner as Imry Llyenthur as he scanned me from filthy, wet hair to my sodden boots.

He gave a bright, toothy, and entirely false smile. "This must be Marend," he said wryly.

"And you must be another of Ramond's fools," I retorted, though my voice came out high and wheezy.

Tdor's eyes rounded. "Marend?" she gasped.

"Keep your distance, traitor," I snapped back.

"Hearing that word from *you* makes me sick," Ramond exclaimed behind me. I whipped around to face this new enemy.

His fists clenched, and his face mottled with rage and the desire for action.

"Ramond," said the blond newcomer.

"Augh." Ramond groaned as he backed away. "When I think how *close*—"

"Yecch!" Tdor honked. "Look! Marend, what happened?"

Increasing dizziness made it curiously difficult to see even in the light. Even familiar faces lost their recognizable characteristics, blurring into round eyes, all staring at the floor at my feet.

I dropped my head to look.

Mistake. The dizziness lurched wildly when I saw the blood dripping into the pooling water around my boots. I jerked my head up again, but it was too late. The last things I saw were the gray-blue eyes of the newcomer, who sat there, leg swinging back and forth, while I collapsed like a sack of stones.

Eleven

I WOKE TO FIND myself lying in a narrow bed in a small room, wearing nothing but drawers and singlet. My shoulder had been bandaged.

The walls around my bed were rough-plastered and washed with a yellowy white. A tiny table, barely big enough for a meal tray, sat against a wall, next to a ladder-backed chair. The far wall had a small window high up. It was open; from beyond burbled running water.

Where was I? And more important, in whose hands? A headache throbbed behind my eyes when I lifted my head. There was no escape through that window, which was about the size of my head, and I could see that the door had no latch on this side. The room smelled a bit of dust, and some other scents difficult to identify. Paint? Yes—though the tile floor was clean-swept, I saw markings where boxes had been stacked.

This had once been a servant's room, given a sturdy door and repurposed to a storeroom, and now repurposed again as a cell.

I lay back, shut my eyes against the headache, and dozed off, waking when the bar lifted on the other side of the door, squeaked, and the door swung open. A girl of about sixteen elbowed her way in and set down a tray as she eyed me. Then she said gravely, "Do you think you could eat something, Marend?"

"Just bring me my clothes if you want to be helpful." My voice came out hoarse. "And if you don't, get lost."

She turned, a dark brown braid swinging out before she slipped through the door, and the bar slammed into place with a loud *wham*.

I flipped up the back of my hand to the door, but then I forgot her when I felt the sides of the jug on the tray. Water! I didn't bother pouring any into the waiting cup, but drank straight from the jug. Then sat back, my stomach sloshing.

Next to the jug sat a plate of plain bread-and-cheese. I forced down the impulse to attack it, remembering having read somewhere that after going without food for days it was not wise to eat fast, or a lot.

I took a small bite. Either it was the best bread ever made, or else hunger made the rye tangy, the crust crisp, the bread itself still warm. The cheese's sharpness complemented the rye, with a smooth under-taste of wild herb. I meant to eat only a little, and wait to evaluate the effect, but before I knew it the plate was empty and I thumbed up every vestige of a crumb.

Then sank back and shut my eyes.

A very short time after there was a sharp rap, followed by a male voice. "I'm coming in."

Crossly I sat up, ignoring the head-throb, and yanked the blankets around me as I leaned against the wall.

The door opened again, but it was not the teen. A young man of medium height walked in. There was something vaguely familiar about the cut of his cheekbones and his forehead. His wavy blond hair was cut in the military style, but he wore the shapeless clothing of a laborer, the undyed shirt sporting old clay stains. A potter? A potter who knew how to fight: I recognized him as my assailant on the roof. His lip curled as we took one another in.

He began conversationally, "I've been bored for a week with yap about you and your antics. Having known and respected your father, I wondered how he could possibly have managed to turn out a pompous and conceited twit of a daughter."

Conceited?

Astonishment made anger impossible for a heartbeat. That word had no meaning in reference to *me!*

"Especially when he had spoken so highly of you. He cannot have known about this single-minded feud you've been pursuing with Ramond Vendren. Two teens died in your gang warfare. Two lives snuffed out, two families grieved, and all because of your temper tantrum over an insult from a boy still growing his two front teeth."

"It wasn't like that," I snapped back. "I mean, yes, he insulted me. But it wasn't just me he insulted. Ramond also said Rom wouldn't be taken by the academy, on account of his leg. Sindan, because of the eye accident, when he was little. We proved we were just as good as the academy cadets. We strove to be better."

"By fighting each other?"

"We were scrapping—"

He cut me off. "You were fighting. When two people die it's a fight."

"But that was an accident—"

Again he cut me off. "How long were you going to persist in this feud? Ramond Vendren says he tried to get you to end it. The greengrocer twins corroborated that. If Norsunder hadn't torn up the city first, were you planning to divide it? Fill the streets with blood instead?"

"No!" But as I said it, I knew that though I hadn't intended that outcome, the feud had been so necessary to me that it might have gone that way.

"How can I believe that?" he retorted. "I've never heard of anyone turning traitor so easily. Tell me! Will you believe anything I say, and follow me blindly, if I pitchfork you a few loads of horseshit about how great you are?"

I wanted to attack him, but my head panged, driving me back in my tangled blanket.

He got up and moved to the door. "That's enough for now. I'll leave you to sulk. By the way, the people here have gone to a lot of trouble to house you. I suggest you curb your rudeness, or you're going to get it right back from me."

"Give me my clothes and I'll take myself off."

"Straight to Imry Llyenthur to continue licking his heels? No. You're going to stay right there, and you're going to do nothing but talk to me, whenever I have the time, and the patience, to listen to it. We'll see about some clothes."

The door shut behind him. Wham! The bar dropped on the other side.

Despite the headache and the shoulder I jumped up

and tested the window. It was just as small as I'd thought, set well into the thick stone of the wall.

I stood on tiptoe and craned my neck, trying to see over the edge. All I could glimpse was a sliver of rushing water, a bit of shrubbery, and a lot of sky.

I collapsed back on the bed, rolled up in the blankets.

After another nap, the door opened again. I stiffened my shoulders, hiding a flinch —

It was the girl. "I brought you some soup, milk." She set crockery on the table, reached behind the door, and was handed something. "And something to wear."

I eyed the bundle of dull blue material, revolted. "What about *my* clothes?"

"They were ruined. We burned them. This is all we can spare. May I look at that bandage?"

I sat up and turned my back. "Those rips could have been fixed."

"By you? No one here has the time. Oh, good." A feather-light touch along the edges of my bandage. "I'd hoped it would scab up nicely. That means we got it clean. It'll heal rapidly now."

I shrugged. "Hardly feel it. Who are you?"

"Lnand," she said softly, then shut the door. And bolted it.

I ate the thick soup, drained the milk, and realized the headache was diminishing. My stomach had even stopped churning. I forced my attention to the unpromising blue bundle. Just as I suspected, it turned out to be a cotton-linen robe with a worn sash through loops.

Mother-clothes.

I flung it on the floor, climbed back in bed, and since I had no candle, when darkness closed in I fell back to sleep.

Right after dawn lifted the shadows from the little room Lnand woke me. She set down a tray on the table, checking when she saw the robe on the floor. She left without speaking to me.

I got out of bed, kicked the robe away, sat down and ate. I was ravenous. Since I was alone I even licked the bowl after I ate the oatmeal drizzled with honey, and I thumbed up every morsel of the cornbread. Last I devoured the poached egg, drank down the coffee, and wished there had been more.

When the bolt scraped, I hopped back into bed. I pulled up the covers and turned my back.

Lnand picked up the tray (I heard the rattle of dishes), and said from the doorway, "When the door opens next, you'll have a visitor, and I am going to take the blanket to be washed."

Right.

Hating her, and the world, I got up and wrestled into the robe, so angry I half-enjoyed the pull of the scabs over my wound. The pain made me feel vindicated somehow.

The robe was much too large, a humiliating reminder of my size that harrowed up all the old anger again. At least my mother-clothes had fit. I looked down at the dragging hem. The waist loops hit the bottom of my hips. I tied the sash anyway.

About a bell into the morning watch, the potter returned as Lnand had threatened, Lnand right behind him to take the begrimed blanket away.

This time the potter was carrying some paper and a pair of scissors. I readied for a comment about the accursed robe, but he paid no attention to what I was wearing.

"Good morning, Marend, how do you feel?" he said. His tone was cheery. Too cheery. I eyed him suspiciously. "Not talking? Well. I've brought you something to do, to help alleviate the boredom." He held up the paper and scissors.

"Are you Imry Llyenthur's brother?" I demanded.

"No." He snorted a laugh. "Mentioned him, did he? Llyenthur's brother is, I hope, safely out of the country. I owe him a big favor for diverting Imry so we could pinch you."

As he spoke, he began folding a paper into a sort of wide fan.

"Llyenthur said something about Detlev."

"Ah!" The potter's brows went up. "Did he!"

"What's that supposed to mean?"

"I didn't know Detlev lent a hand. If he did." A grin. "Now, watch. I haven't much in the way of artistic ability, but if you cut the little shapes right…" He began very carefully to snip at the folded paper with the scissors, pausing once or twice to glance up at me. "Don't want to talk? Then you can listen. When I was small, I was under the thumb of a horseapple of a guardian. He went through a phase when I was, oh, about ten, of sticking me in the dungeon whenever I seriously annoyed him. Which was pretty often. Ostensibly these stays were to clear my mind but actually they were a reminder of who gave the orders. There's not much to do in a dungeon, so I learned — this." He dropped the scissors on the table, picked apart the fan, and revealed a row of paper-warriors. "There! Not bad, eh? And it's been years since I made the last one." He smiled proudly.

I stared at him. Was I in the hands of a madman?

He laid the row of paper-warriors on the table. "He'd come in, find the walls festooned, and the sheer inanity of it used to make him nearly dance with rage. Anyway, cutting 'em out was fun, and took time, particularly if you designed variations, so I thought I'd offer you this harmless but pleasant diversion for your hours of solitude."

Hope burned in me, but I kept my face blank. "You're going to leave — that stuff?" I didn't dare to say the word *scissors*.

"Yes," he said brightly. "Have I hit upon something you'll enjoy?"

I gave him my bland mother-smile, enjoying the mental image of him dead on the floor with the scissors in his chest, and myself free.

"Is there anything else you'd like to know?" he asked.

"Yeah. This place in Methden?"

"Nah."

"Ah." I'd thought the air smelled different somehow, but I wasn't sure just how. Different growing things, maybe? "Where?"

"I'll tell you later," he said. "Anything else?"

I eyed him, assessing him for later attack. Medium height — not as tall as my father had been. Still, at least two palm-breadths taller than me, curse it. And I remembered he knew how to fight.

I said, "That was Llyenthur's way, to let me ask questions."

"It's a common technique. The questions sometimes

give as much information to the one as the answers do to the other. And I'm using it now. So tell me, what's on your mind?"

"Getting out of here."

"What would you do then?"

"That's my affair, not yours."

"I can probably guess. I think I'll take myself off now, but here's a topic of discussion for our next meeting. As you contemplate the rows of little warriors you make, why don't you consider which approach makes the better leader: one who learns each person's weaknesses and strengths in order to best place them, or one who trains them into a similar fast-actioned but non-thinking unit? Have a good time." He left.

The scissors and paper were on the table. I laughed.

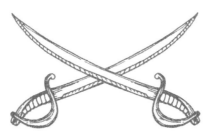

Twelve

LNAND BROUGHT ME SOME lunch, and a watch later some dinner, along with the clean blanket. I was not really hungry for the dinner, but I forced myself to down every bite, thinking of a possibly long hike ahead of me once I got past the potter and escaped.

I flexed my arms, and slowly did some exercises, ignoring the tweaks and twinges from my shoulder. The cut had barely broke the surface of my skin. My strength was fast returning. If only I didn't have that stupid robe hampering my legs!

The scissors were under my pillow. When the rap on the door came at last, I sat up ready and waiting. Just before nightfall — what could be better? I closed my hands around the scissors and stood up against the wall, just out of sight of the opening door, poised on the edge of the bed so I could use flying weight.

The door swung in — and I launched!

A breathless, painful whirl of limbs, two thumps of my heart, and a single breath later I lay face down on my bed, nose squashed into the clean blanket, which smelled of sunshine, a knee across the backs of my legs.

A hand like steel pinned my wrists against my back, keeping me immovable while fingers P-R-I-E-D the scissors from my fist.

"Thank you," he said when he had them, as though I'd presented them to him with a curtsey and a dimple instead of hanging on with all my strength.

The blanket got hot and stuffy with my face mashed into it. I readied myself to try again the moment he let me

up, but as he held me there, my arms aching, I got hold of
my temper enough to realize that if my planned attack got
me nowhere, another try would be useless.

The instant I thought that, the hand and knee lifted. I
got up and irritably straightened the robe out as he wiped
his hair back, pocketed the scissors, and sat down.

"It's impossible to do *anything* in a robe," I muttered,
though I knew I'd plain been outmatched.

"I suppose it's got its drawbacks. I've not been called
on to test 'em," he acknowledged.

"The times you've worn robes?" I said, just to be nasty.

He grinned. "The one time I dressed in a robe, I was
acting pretty sedate."

This took me by surprise. "You've disguised as a *girl?*"

"Yep. Not recently, but then until the Norsundrians
elected to make their appearance I haven't seen much
action for a couple years." He smothered a laugh. My
expression must have been a combination of amazement
and revulsion. "Now, don't think I was lauded for my
grace and beauty, but then I haven't been handed any
white roses for beauty as myself, either. I'm sorry about the
scissors. I guess I should have foreseen the temptation
would be irresistible. At any rate I don't see the walls
festooned with cheery groupings of little warriors. Ah,
perhaps one of the things that made it so enjoyable for me
when I was a prisoner was my guardian's considerable
annoyance. I guess I robbed you of that by suggesting it
myself. So tell me. Did you think about our topic of
discussion?"

"No. But I'd say both."

"That is, sadly, correct. And here I was looking forward to taking the opposite view to yours so we could
argue."

I realized I couldn't guess his age. In certain light and
angles he looked a few years older than I was, and in others
a lot older. His eyes looked old partially because they had
marks of tiredness under them, and partly because most of
his real expression was in his eyes. His mouth either
grinned or looked sarcastic.

When he raised his hand to lay aside the scissors I saw
faint but unmistakable rope-burn scars on his wrists.

"You ride with the army?" I asked. "Seen action?"

"I never made it to recruit. But I've seen my share of action."

"What can you do?"

"What do you mean, martial arts?" He raised and wiggled a forefinger.

"Yep."

He glanced up at the window as if to think. "I'm adequate with knives, barely competent with a sword, and reasonably reliable with a bow. You?"

His tone somehow made it impossible to brag. "I can shoot."

"With all your training?"

"I'm great—against teens," I said shortly. Then I remembered. "And I know everyone's skills. Was that *you* who shot Norgiem, that night?"

He flicked his fingers out. "I must say, even I was impressed," he said modestly. "Angle, rain, distance were all against me. Definitely one of my best."

I couldn't help a laugh. "Now that's what *I* call conceit—" Then all those words flooded back, and my anger kindled again, and I couldn't bring myself to ask the most important question: had Retren survived?

The potter glanced at the window. "Light's nearly gone. Shall I get a candle, and we can talk some more, or have you had enough of me for one day?"

"What'll get me out of here sooner?"

"I don't know!"

I made a noise of disgust.

"See you tomorrow." He smiled. And left.

I spent the rest of the day alternately exercising until my muscles trembled, and lying in a heap on the bed, hating everything and everybody.

The next morning Lnand said as she put my breakfast down, "I've been trying to find you another robe, but no one really has any extra clothes, and cloth is hard to trade for these days."

I said, "Ask the boys. I'd rather wear a shirt and riding pants."

"I'll ask, but it seems no one has anything to spare. I

did think of a thing, though, when you want your robe washed. Usually we put clothes outside the door at night, and whoever's on laundry-duty collects them, and we put them folded outside the door next morning. I thought you could tell me at dinner, and I'd come back at night, get it, and bring it to you with your breakfast."

"What about cleaning frames?"

"We don't have one."

"Fine. But if a wearable shirt or trousers turn up, I want to put in first dibs. Somebody else can have this thing." I jerked my thumb at that robe, which was completely innocent of ribbons or other courtly furbelows, but existed as a reminder.

She turned up her palm and went to the door.

"Are you a servant?" I asked, because she didn't have the manner of one.

"No." Her face colored as she paused at the door. "But I was the only one —" She flushed a deeper red.

"Willing? Is that it? To have anything to do with me? What do they think, my touch will turn them into Norsundrians? What rabbits!"

"Sorry," she said softly, and left hastily.

When the potter turned up I snapped, "What's this horseshit about the servants, or whoever they are, being afraid of me? I'm not exactly armed."

"Do you want them to be afraid of you?"

"Yes! No." My face burned. "Not that. Not really."

Unexpectedly, he said, "It sounds like what you want is respect."

"Yes," I exclaimed. "That's it exactly. Is that so bad?"

"Everyone wants respect. Including your rival Ramond. And the young woman who generously volunteered to bring your meals. Something you might contemplate in your leisure moments. Another thing to consider is that the others here are not afraid of you, but nobody wants to be around a sulker with rude manners."

"Manners!" I scoffed. "I no longer feel it necessary to put up with that hypocrisy."

"Being polite evolved so people could live in proximity with one another. Which some would rate more highly than scrabbling one's way over a pile of corpses to a position of power. Never mind, you obviously don't agree.

Shall we discuss instead what's wrong with making efforts to render life more pleasant? Should life be nasty, brutish, and short for the majority so the winner of the power struggle can have a life that's nasty, brutish, and long? Unless he too gets nailed by the next promising comer?"

"I suppose it depends on what you call pleasant," I said with a lifetime's worth of pent-up hate. "I don't consider dragging around in heavy, stuffy clothing pleasant, or dousing one's hair or clothes in perfumes that remind one of a sick-room, or cawing over the pointless mawkishness of art. Pleasure is a hard ride in cold weather, in the achievement of a plan—in *winning*."

"No argument from me. Although we might define that 'winning'—later. I'll try instead to appeal to your common sense. Let's talk about the Norsundrian hierarchy. Are you so naïve you expect the Norsundrians move smoothly up the ranks, promoted on a merit system? In a place where 'retirement' is meaningless, and death can be another form of slavery?"

I was ready to repeat what Llyenthur had said, but now I began to wonder if what he had told me was far too easy. "I saw none of what you say."

"Of course not. You probably saw Llyenthur's minions saluting smartly, underscoring his rank, but you never saw what he did to get there. And I'll wager anything you care to name that he did not show you any of Norsunder's trouble spots, either."

Again, I remembered my annoyance when I gave the order and saw no response until the words *Llyenthur says*.

"To pick up where we left off, we were discussing Imry Llyenthur's probable motivations for recruiting you. Consider how much of a blow it would be to the rest of the kingdom to hear that Jarl of Methden's daughter went over to the Norsundrians of her own free will, and then purged her own city of its best resistors. He's at an impasse now. He can either send the butchers in, and chances are pretty good he'd end up with a demolished populace even more set against him, or continue to deal with constant covert resistance."

"We discussed that," I cut in.

"I'll bet he didn't discuss how much fun it was for him to play mental games with you."

"Fun?"

"Fun to Imry Llyenthur is pinning a small creature to a wall by a knife and cheering on its efforts to get free. Which is what he did in spirit, if not in fact, to you and your family."

"That's not true," I retorted. "I see I may have made some mistakes, but everything I did was my decision, from beginning to end."

His reaction to that was odd. Neither belief nor disbelief, but disappointment. "Admitting that is a virtue, eh? Well, you're only half right, but never mind."

I remembered that mood I'd been in after Imry's tour. Remembering that exultation—not quite exaltation, though I'd considered it so at the time—frightened me a little. As I wrestled mentally, he was silent, staring up at the little window. Then there was a soft knock at the door.

"Marend, I have your lunch," Lnand called.

"I'll leave you in peace," he said, and got up.

"Wait." It was out before I could consider.

He paused at the door. "Yes?"

My face burned as all the old nastiness churned inside me. But I forced the words out anyway. "My brother. Is he..."

"Alive." He said the one word, and the door shut behind him.

Lnand returned a short while later. I said to her, "If it's so hard to get cloth, why were my clothes burned? I would've mended them. I hate doing it, but I do know how. Something to do."

"I wasn't there," she muttered, not looking at me. "I just know they were." She closed the door.

I picked at the food, then exercised feverishly, trying to work off the restlessness. How odd it was! My mind used to be clear. I knew what I wanted, I considered my resources, planned a strategy, and acted on it! Now trying to think was like picking at dark river-ice. Every time I tried to force my way past the ice, my insides churned and surged again. It took all my concentration to get that under control.

If only I could get outside in the clean air! Except I could feel a steady flow of air through that stone window, whose shutter had been flung wide. Also, I had been taught better than that. I ought to be able to think anywhere, and outside I'd just be distracted.

I picked up the chair, and tried to resolve the rest-lessness by using it as a weight, then I stretched. While my body was busy, I tried to order my thoughts. Begin with the first and worst accusation. What's the first? The potter — what was his name — had said —

The first, and worst, was his statement that I had been easily convinced to move against my own side.

No. By far, the worst was that I had very nearly killed my brother.

There was the gnawing again. I sat on the bed, my arms pressed across my middle. It seemed impossible, and yet memory was merciless: I had raised my hand in the signal. But for the raid, I would have done something from which there was no turning back.

Easily, the potter had said so disdainfully.

Perhaps Imry really *had* enchanted me? No, I'd have been aware of magic messing with my mind, surely? "Easily."

Easy for you to say, I wanted to scream at him. Because Imry Llyenthur was the *only* person who recognized, and offered me, what I had wanted my whole life. Anger boiled up, again, the righteous anger, the kind that felt good, because it convinced me I was justified in my actions, which gave me strength.

Thirteen

I WAS STILL PILING up arguments for the potter when he returned, which was not long after Lnand brought me the evening meal.

"What do I call you?" I said the moment he walked in the door.

"Van will do," he said with a slight shrug.

"Van what?"

"Just that, for now."

"There must be a wing of Vans within arrow-shot. Indevan being the most common name in the kingdom, my father once told me, because the last king was so popular. Who is your family? Anyone I know?"

"My family is irrelevant right now."

"Are you wanted by the Norsundrians?" I asked in disbelief, because why would anyone want a potter, until the obvious struck me. That military haircut—clearly he was wearing a disguise. I looked him up and down, and yes, there under the worn hem of the laborer's trousers were the squared toes and the high heels of cavalry boots. A pair very well worn. Yet he'd said he hadn't ridden in the army. A lie? Or could he be one of the king's agents?

"Did the Norsundrians do that?" I indicated his wrists.

He blinked at his wrists as though he'd forgotten those scars. "Yes. They did indeed. Years ago."

I said, "Well, Van, you're right. I was a fool to believe that blabbermouth Imry Llyenthur. I see it now. And if you'll let me out of here, I'm on my way back to Methden to start making up for it."

"Revenge, you mean? What would you do, shoot a

Norsundrian for every year of your life? Or Llyenthur's, perhaps?"

"As a start. And I'll go from there. I'm not afraid of action, and I'm going to show that birdwit I know plenty about discipline, action, and command, without being a Norsundrian."

Van spread his hands and looked down at them for a long breath.

"You don't believe me," I said shortly.

He looked up, his face absolutely serious. "I do believe you. And I might prove to be wrong, but I'm not going to let you go."

"Why?"

"Because—at best—you've gone back to where you were two months ago. Look, Marend, I apologize heartily for all the things I said to you at first. I know quite well that sarcasm is a weapon that cuts both ways, and I used it anyway. Though I nearly always regret it after." He added that with an odd sort of smile, more pained than humorous. "Part of my motivation was, I thought if I started out more hard-nosed than Llyenthur'd made you, I'd get your attention faster. And I'd agreed with your gang when we planned the snatch that we'd only keep you locked up until you'd shaken the Norsundrian influence. But there still remains the reason you got that way. Because he didn't really make you that way, did he? He just sped up a process he saw already going on, and turned it to his advantage."

My anger flared up again. "You think I hopped the fence just because he told me I was smart! It wasn't that. Well, that was a part. He got me on his side because he didn't act like he saw a *little girl*." I could barely choke out the words that had galled me for so many years—not just because Ramond had flung them at me, though that had had its effect, but because my father had used them first. Reasonably. Even fondly. But unanswerably.

"When Llyenthur saw me, he said, he saw a commander. All I ever wanted. My entire life. Was to follow in my da's command." My voice shook. I shut my mouth so hard my teeth clicked.

Van gazed at the window, his expression remote. Finally he said, "Can you see that Llyenthur said what you most wanted to hear?"

"But he was making it true!"

Van turned his palm flat in negation. "He was only setting you up. No, don't argue yet. Think, first. He's still struggling to control Marloven Hess. Do you truly believe he's going to leave a fourteen-year-old in command of the southern border, whether a girl your size, or a boy as tall as a pine?"

I opened my mouth to protest, but I remembered that patrol, the little signs of insubordination. After I'd had to use Llyenthur's name to summon them. "Why would he even bother?" My voice shook again, and I flushed.

"Malice is the easy answer. A game is probably closer to the mark. Remember what I said about the effect on the rest of the kingdom hearing that the Jarl of Methden's daughter had gone over to Norsunder? That, too."

I flinched.

If Van saw it, he ignored it, and returned to gazing out the tiny window (which was easy for him, I noticed bitter-ly—*he* did not have to stand on tiptoe) as he continued. "There are rumors that he's set up various experiments, mostly with young people, all over. It's long-term plan-ning. But that's a side issue right now. We're only guessing."

He turned back. "When I was exactly the same age as you, I had similar expectations, though perhaps for diff-erent reasons, that my gaining command would solve all the rest of my problems. Which is why I'm so reluctant to let you go back to Methden now."

I hissed a sigh.

He gave me a wry smile very different from that toothy, mocking grin. "Sorry. I'll try to make this as clear as I can. If you will in your turn answer a question. Did you know when your father reported those two teens' deaths several years ago, he didn't quite tell the truth about the matter?"

"Yes." Ah, an agent, then? Who else would see a Jarl's reports? "He told me he was going to report it to the king as an accidental clash between some itinerant roughs and some local trouble-makers. He told me that before giving me the beating of a lifetime. He said from then on it was *my* responsibility if anyone was seriously injured. So I thought up the yellow chalk marks on defeated opponents. And no more died!"

"I heard about that," he said grimly. "An inspiration in humiliation tactics. No wonder the feud lasted as long as it did. Anyway, did you think your father, who was usually extremely honest, had done the right thing? You know about your grandfather, right?"

"Oh yes. That's why the beating. He said we were still living down the humiliation of my grandfather's traitorous end."

"Did your brother get thrashed, too?"

"Not as much as I did," I said bitterly. "Retren was perfect," I said, the words still coming out bitter. I hadn't meant them to. I cleared my throat and tried again. "He never did anything wrong."

"Have you forgotten the slaps?"

"Slaps?"

"Did your father not give you permission to slap Retren any time he admitted that he did not want to attend the academy?"

I shrugged. "Those were just slaps. For laziness and cowardice! Why else would anyone not want to go, when they didn't even have to compete, but would be invited?" I thought back, and added, "I know they were hard slaps. Sometimes. But that was because he made me so angry. And anyway he stopped saying it, and I stopped slapping him, as ordered."

"As ordered," Van breathed. Then his tone changed. "Were you aware that you were invited to the academy?"

"Of course I was," I said scornfully. "A pity invite. But Father said that he would not permit me to be the bottom of the class, scragged by bullies when the instructors and the radlavs weren't around. He said it would be cruel to me, and would make Methden a laughingstock. We have to be tough, sharing border protection with South Army..." I faltered there, my throat thick when I remembered what had happened to South Army at Aladas Pass. There was no more South Army.

I stiffened my back. "Father said that if I gained more stature, and learned to excel, he would reconsider." I stopped—I couldn't bear to say anything about the agony of self-hatred I endured when each season Mother ordered new shoes exactly the same size as my old ones, because I was not growing, whereas Retren's feet had gotten longer than mine when he was nine.

I couldn't see Van's face because he was rubbing his eyes with thumb and forefinger. His hand dropped suddenly, and in the fading light I saw the marks of tiredness there. "I can't think any more. I'll see you in the morning."

"Why the lack of rest? On watch for a raid?"

"Yes and no. But mostly I've been kept up at night by a roommate with sleep problems."

"Roommate?"

His lip curled. "You're the only one with private quarters. Everyone else is crowded."

"Where is this place?"

"Tell you what. Maybe I'll show you in the morning. There was some talk of a picnic. You and I might take a walk, and wouldn't be interrupted."

That meant getting out of that room! "Where are my boots? They haven't been burned — or appropriated?" I added, remembering Lnand's comment on the scarcity of clothing.

"No. They're right outside the door."

"Did *you* make them burn my duds? There was something funny in Lnand's voice and her face when she told me."

He blinked. "Me? What interest do I have in someone's clothes? Of course I didn't!"

He sounded so genuinely astonished I didn't realize until later his tone made it sound like it was news to him. And yet he'd been the one to say *we'll get you some clothes*, not *we'll get your clothes*.

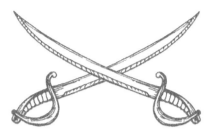

Fourteen

I WOKE FILLED WITH eagerness. I was going to leave that room!

I had to laugh at myself, excited over so small a thing.

That wasn't the true cause of that sense of anticipation. Van had mentioned a picnic. I figured I might be seeing (or glimpsing) the gang, but the one I truly wanted to see was Retren.

I woke that morning aware, for the first time, that in all the days that had passed he had not come to visit me. Why not? I wasn't sick—that first day or two had been recovery. It had always been me having to go visit him during all his various illnesses. Maybe it didn't occur to him, as I'd never been sick a day in my life. He could at least have poked his head in.

Resentment began to stir in me, but the moment it did, my mind shot back to the last time I saw Retren, when my guts were churning with boiling nails and shards of glass, and he had lifted his head, staring straight at me as I raised my—

I'd managed to mentally sidestep that for the past few days. Nothing had happened; Van had said he was alive. But the impact hit me fully: he would not have been. If I had had my way, the sun would have come up today, exactly as it had, but Retren would not have opened his eyes to it. He would have been dead tonight, and next year, and thereafter—dead before he turned eleven. Dead no matter how much I wanted to go back, just as Da was dead. Only Retren wouldn't have died fighting the enemy, surrounded by piles of Norsundrians whose lives he had taken. He would have been dead *by my command.*

Llyenthur might have lied about a lot of things, or twisted them, but that one was inescapably true: he had stood right beside me, his hands behind his back. It was I who gave that signal.

The more my mind flooded with memory of that night's images, the sounds, even the smell of rain on stone and a whiff of moss from the north wall, the worse the gnawing sensation inside me intensified. I had to sit on the bed, my forearms pressed against my gut, as I fought for control. Only then could I eat the breakfast Lnand brought, though the boiled oats were congealed by the time I could let go.

When she came for the tray, she brought my boots and socks. I jammed into them, my knee jiggling up and down, until Van opened the door. I leaped to my feet—forgetting the damned robe hem, and nearly pitched onto my face. I caught myself painfully against the wall, and impatiently yanked handfuls of robe through the sash, to slop over.

Van waited. When I was done, I eyed him, and caught a suspicious quirk at one corner of his mouth. "You're laughing at me," I snarled.

"Nope. Nope. Nope," he lied, his voice unsteady. "But I will admit that really looks terrible."

I couldn't suppress a groan as I looked down at myself, and the swags of fabric lumping over the sagging sash, with my boots sticking out below. "I really wish someone hadn't gone and tossed my clothes into the fire just because they didn't want to wash them. I would have done it," I muttered.

Van's smile vanished, his expression bland. "Before we go out, I want you to establish a mind-shield."

"A mind-shield?"

"You don't know what that is? I believe orders went out some time ago, requiring the jarls to see that people were instructed, in case we found ourselves in the situation we are in now."

"Oh, he did. And we learned to imagine a brick wall in our minds. But he said it was mostly foolery, like magic. Something for weak outland lighters and the like."

"Nevertheless. We're not leaving this room until I'm satisfied with yours, because you can be sure Imry

Llyenthur is trying to find you, when he has time between all his other pursuits, and your thoughts are like a mad bull bellowing in the field and scaring the crows the next mountain over. He would not have to try very hard to find you."

I sighed loudly, and imagined a brick wall — then something flicked my mind, like an ear flick, only from the inside. It didn't hurt as much as the brief, dismissive inward rap from that bearded man in the fancy room — that had been more like being smacked with a stick inside the skull. But this stung, and I yelped, "Ouch!"

"Do it right. Or we're not stepping outside this room."

"How did you learn that trick? Is that one of the things they teach you in the capital?" I muttered.

He merely waited. So I set about putting mental bricks down, keeping my thoughts inside what I built, and avoiding looking out. It took concentration because I'd lose track if my mind wandered. Frustrated and impatient, I gritted my teeth and kept at it. And I sensed another of those flicks, but it hit my wall — which vanished.

"That was good, but you have to maintain it. Again."

I built, he did his trick, I held on.

"Good enough. But I want you to practice. From now on, those zaps can come at any time."

I sighed, but didn't utter any of the curses I wanted to, because I was afraid he'd refuse to let me out. But then he opened his hand toward the door, and I couldn't get out fast enough.

The place was a big, rambling pottery farm. He took me into every production room, and explained how they made most of the crockery in the warm months, then fired and painted it in the cold months, gathered underground around the kiln where it was warm and dry. I found the tour more interesting than I'd thought I would, once I got over my disappointment that we were not in a secret military camp.

The owner and Master Artist, a woman named Nalenda, was originally from Parayid, way down south. But I'm not going to record it all; it's not my purpose, and it was all so new that I can't remember all the details.

I will say, after hearing of all the work that went into the dishes I ate off of, I appreciated them more.

We spent a good part of an hour touring the inside rooms, then went out to inspect the clay beds, and stacks and stacks of drying pottery, etc. Then we went and sat on the roof of the low, rambling main building. The sun was bright, and my flapping robe at least had had summer sleeves, so I didn't chill in spite of a brisk wind.

Hills rolled away to my left, and the border-mountains near Methden were a far and hazy line to the west. And, to the east, on rising ground, a rough dark line—"That's Darchelde, isn't it?" I asked Van.

He turned up his hand, then leaned back, shutting his eyes.

I studied the long line of the forest. I'd never been there, of course—had never been outside of Methden. I'd never wanted to go outside the city, except to the academy.

"If they're really short on clothes, why don't I go home, steal mine, and bring 'em back. I can send this thing back." I plucked at the awful robe.

"Best if you don't return to Methden," he said, eyes still closed.

"Why not? If you think *I'm* afraid of facing Imry again—"

"If you're not, you're crazy. You should be. Of course, it's possible I feel that way because I'm afraid. You know what'll happen if he gets his sticky mitts on you again?" He opened his eyes, which were usually more gray than blue, except out here in the rain-washed sunlight, they were more blue than gray.

"Execution—"

"Nope. Enchant your brains out, and have you pick up where you left off."

"He said they don't have loyalty spells."

"They don't. That doesn't mean there aren't far more unpleasant methods of messing with your mind. Anyway, you're much more useful to him as a symbol than as a person. News of you hopping the fence would hurt Stad, wherever he is. And the jarls—"

"And the king?" I asked, half in disbelief. I could not grasp my sudden leap from *little girl*, a nonentity, to this kind of importance. But I sensed he was right. "Symbols. He talked about how useful they are."

"His game—one of his games—is to force you to focus

on the symbol, rather than on what it represents. Then he destroys the symbol."

"Now that I know it, I'll be able to remember that, and ignore him."

"I don't think so. Knowing it, recognizing exactly what he's doing, only prolongs the process, especially when he keeps at it."

"Symbols are stupid," I said.

He laughed. "So's horseshit and runny noses."

"Those are—oh, I see what you're saying. Part of life. Maybe. I guess I was never interested in all those so-called beautiful symbols my mother yammered on about."

"Of course not." He sat up, and grinned. "Did Llyenthur ever mention 'em to you?"

"N-no. Actually he did, but in a way that put my mother in one place, and me and him united in looking down on her and her silly things."

"Divide and conquer. He cut you off from her, insinuating how clever you were to despise her, I'll bet you anything."

"He did." My mind ranged past that to the things he said about Retren, but I kept my teeth clenched against that realization.

"Then he used your personal symbols."

"What? I don't have any—"

"Your black clothes, the color and make of the night maneuvers gear at the academy, and—"

I scoffed, "That's just practical—"

"And your father."

That silenced me, as Retren's words came back, *That's just what you do with Da*—and with them, the anger. "You think I was trying to make him into a new father?" I sneered.

"I thought we were talking about symbols," Van remarked to the sky, hands laced behind his head and one foot crossed over the other.

My insides surged again. I struggled hard against it. "Symbols," I said. "My father wasn't any symbol, he was my *father*."

"Guess again," Van said, watching four swifts streak across the sky, then plunge toward a distant clump of budding trees.

I kept my teeth clenched for two or three long breaths, then vented the air in a rush when the gut churning began to hurt. "You don't know me. You don't know *Da.*"

Van sighed, his face turned up to the sun. "Let's talk about Llyenthur."

"What about?" Van gave me nothing to attack, and after a flash of annoyance, the urge to attack faded away.

"Tell me what he did when he first made his appearance. That is, the first things that made you aware of him."

I shrugged. "I don't know. I thought at first he was just some flunky."

"Try."

I remembered my terrible rage at discovering Imry Llyenthur had settled himself into the tower. "He moved into my father's office. Thirty empty rooms in the castle, and he has to pick that one!"

"Why d'you think he did that?"

Stuff like *Because it overlooks the garrison — because it keeps warriors from trampling the lovely carpets in the residence,* went through my mind, to be dismissed. Those were Da's reasons, in honor of Mother's wishes, and I was reasonably certain that Mother would not have told Llyenthur to spare her imported Bermundi carpets. "Because it was my father's," I said. "So he makes the obvious point to everyone that Da's gone, and he's there."

"Not to everyone. Most of Methden probably thought your father took care of army work at the garrison command center. If they thought about it at all."

"You can't say he did it just for *me.*"

"Maybe not. It was a move to demonstrate both power and to keep people guessing. But one thing you can be sure of, he knew about you before you think he did."

I opened my mouth to deny it, and remembered the first talk, when he mentioned Sindan and Tdor. "Yes," I said reluctantly. "So?"

"So it's possible he *was* aiming it at you."

"Maybe. Who knows?" I exclaimed impatiently. "What's the purpose of all this conjecture?"

"How'd you feel about him using that tower at the end, when you'd decided to ally with him?"

"Of course I didn't mind, or I wouldn't've agreed!"

"Is it possible—" He turned his head and squinted at

MAREND OF MARLOVEN HESS

me out of one eye " — you felt pretty good about the prospect of that room being turned over to you? Maybe even better about that room than any of the others in the castle you'd shared with your family?"

"Yes, it's true," I said coldly. "So?"

"So think about that. I'll wager a week's dishes duty you were hoping to restore that room to the way your father had had it if and when you took over as Jarlan and Commander. But you weren't going to preserve, say, the family dining room, or the library, or even his rooms he shared with your mother."

"They weren't as important to him, as big a part of his life. He was *happiest* there."

"Nope. You can't sit there and tell me playing garrison commander was more important to him than his family. Equal, maybe, but it was *really* most important to *you*."

"How would you know?"

"I know. I knew your father, remember?"

"Where did you 'know' him? I never saw you before."

"In the king's city. I saw him every year when he made his reports."

"Why, were you one of those desk jockeys the king — "

"We're not talking about me but about your father. Now, why are you getting so wrathful?"

I didn't even realize I was on my feet, standing over him. That rage was boiling inside me again.

I sank down and took a deep breath. I said, "I'd really like to know what you do in the capital. Are you one of the royal desk jockeys?"

"I do work at a desk." He grinned. "And I know 'em all. I take it you don't think much of them?"

"On the contrary! Da told me, he had nothing but contempt when the orders came down assigning one to each Jarl, and nothing but the admitted need for aid with the increased paperwork made him acquiesce. But then he told me when he found out Mordan — our desk jockey — was third in his year at the academy, he knew he'd understand the garrison and so forth. Da became fond of Mordan. We *all* liked him! I remember Da felt reluctant, and sad, when he wanted to go back to his home-province to fight when the Norsundrians came, and we never heard from him again so I guess he bought it."

Van shook his head. "I heard a rumor he's alive, and up to his ears in plots. Of course, I haven't seen him so I can't prove it."

"I'm glad. Amazing, though, how someone so good with a sword, and he is, I saw him in practice, would want to do *paperwork!*"

"Did you ever ask him?"

"No, I thought it might embarrass him."

Van laughed. "Not at all! The desk jockeys chose their jobs because they wanted to do something besides mindlessly swing a sword or march or ride around, and they were chosen because they'd be excellent aides for the commanders should war arise. They wanted a hand in running the country, wanted to see different provinces from home ones, and enjoyed traveling. Did you know why the paperwork started snowing your father's desk, what its purpose was?"

I shrugged. "Da said it was the king's way of curtailing his powers. I thought it would've been less time-consuming (and boring) if Da could go on reporting all that stuff on his yearly visits to the king."

"The paperwork freed your father from having to discuss details on those visits, so they could concentrate on bigger matters. And possible changes. Though your father fought those." Van gave a reminiscent smile. "Everyone knew he would. Looked forward to his trenchant point of view, I think. Though he was conservative—one could say reactionary at times—his reasoning was always well thought out. Listen, Marend, the others are returning. Would you like—ah. Let's go back."

My head had whipped around as I peered down, looking for a small, slight figure with black curly hair. But at the same time I dreaded facing Retren, for every time I thought about him, that terrible image was right back: the last time we saw one another, in that courtyard.

We hopped from the roof to the wall and then down. Neither of us spoke on the walk back inside the U-shaped wing, and down the hall to my room, which after the wide spaces and fresh air looked tinier than ever.

But Van cast me a glance as he paused at the doorway, and in I went.

"Marend," he said, closing the door and sitting down,

"if someone set your foot on fire would you sit around and revile your foot for letting you know it's being crisped, or would you put the fire out, then find out who'd done it and why?"

"What a stupid question!"

"Not if you substitute emotions for the foot."

I began hotly to deny it, but I realized he wouldn't have said anything if he hadn't *seen* it—and it was my own fault for forgetting to blank my face. Irritation overwhelmed me, but I wasn't about to enter into any discussion of emotions, so I said, "How did you know they were coming? I saw nothing."

He tapped his forehead. "Mind-shield, remember? This is why we make them."

I shuddered. "I *hate* that mind stuff."

He sighed dramatically. "And here we spent all these days guarding you should you try to contact Llyenthur."

"*I* can't do it!"

"Contrary, if you concentrated on Llyenthur, he'd find *you*. In fact he's tried a couple of times, but we deflected him."

"Who's we?"

"Couple people here and there—you don't know them—have some ability." He glanced toward the window. "They're back. And I'm on kitchen detail this week, so I have to go. I want to leave you with an important thought, though. Ignoring emotions doesn't work. If you don't deal with them here." He tapped his forehead. "They will get at you any way they can." He tapped his chest and his gut.

I said nothing, eyeing him warily. I was not going to talk about my feelings.

He grinned. "Despite your glare, I'll also add this: people who have good feelings don't despise them."

"That," I said distastefully, "is inane."

"Think about it." He left.

I didn't.

Instead I struggled, all night, against my own anger as that sense that I was justified eroded with every single conclusion I came to.

I tried to argue, and then to think of other things. I thought about mind-contact, and the desk jockeys, and ruling, but that made me realize how very little I knew about anything outside of Methden and its defense.

I thought about some of those histories Llyenthur'd given me, and I saw how I had learned to think of army movement in terms of faceless numbers. But numbers don't bleed. Numbers are tidy—except when I thought of the numbers of our own dead. Each of those numbers was an empty bunk in the garrison, or an empty mat in a house, an empty bed, folded clothes on a shelf. Each with a name. Each with a family who looked at those things, maybe even touched those things, but the warmth of the breathing, speaking, smiling, or frowning person was forever gone.

And that threw me right back to that courtyard, and Retren gazing up at me so steadily as he waited to die.

The hard truth? There was no justification. And though I could blame Llyenthur for saying things that robbed me of sleep for those terrible days, and made me unable to eat, the decision had still been mine.

My mind recoiled, lighting on my outlander nanny, who I hadn't given a thought to for years. My mother had tried herself, and then with the nanny, hired from Mother's own birthplace, to turn my mind away from the garrison, and Da. How I'd detested what I never dignified with the term "lessons."

A pulse of humor banished some of the sickness as I remembered some of my ploys to get rid of her, and eventually (though not without some severe punishments) I won. I made it clear I was tougher and more strong-willed than they'd thought. By then Ret was old enough to make—

And I was right back to the sick, gnawing, churning horror of that courtyard. No. No. I do not want to think about that. I will not think about that. It's over. I lost. And I'm glad I lost. I concentrated on building that mind-shield, brick by brick. Me in this moment on one side. And nothing beyond it, nothing, nothing, *nothing*.

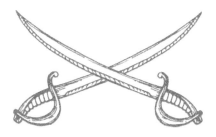

Fifteen

THE NEXT DAY, VAN again approached the question of emotions, and of my father, when I said "Da says" three times in a row, but I retorted angrily that it was coincidence, and anyway as my father'd been my tutor, what could be more natural? Then I retreated behind my mind-shield. He turned the talk to an amusing story about a couple of the pottery children and a flock of venturesome ducklings, while I struggled inwardly to regain command of myself.

He left soon after, but to my surprise, returned that night.

They'd allowed me a candle, which streamed and flickered at his entrance. He said, as the shadows blurred his face, "The others are down in the basement drying room celebrating. It's a pleasant night out. I thought you might like to take a ride."

We saddled two fine horses, then rode out of the farm at a gallop.

There was still a lingering chill of winter in the air, which I found thoroughly exhilarating. We rode fast over unfamiliar ground. I let Van do the leading. I didn't know where we were, of course, and I thought he was going to take us on a long, circuitous route and then back. I didn't care. I just enjoyed something I hadn't been able to do since last autumn.

Then it became clear he was looking for a specific place. He scanned back and forth across the fields until he called, "Over here."

We slowed the horses, and walked them up a small hill crowned by a clump of old, spreading oaks. After we dismounted, he took the reins from my hand and tied them with his over a low branch. At once the horses started lipping at the sweet grass that grew wildly all over the little hill.

"Here."

"What is it we're seeing?"

"Nothing. Have a seat."

We dropped down on the grass. "We're here because it's a pleasant spot, with no one around for an appreciable distance. You can yell and stamp and shout to your heart's content and no one but me and the horses will hear."

"What?" I demanded, and got up again.

He held out a hand. "I'm between you and the horses, you'll note, and I think you know you won't get past me."

"What *is* this?" I said in my coldest voice.

"Possibly one of the biggest mistakes of a long and venerable career of mistakes." He sighed. "Look, Marend, you're too much like I was some years ago, and we're not the only ones in this country. I've got to try, for a number of reasons I won't go into yet. I think this is the best way."

"Try what?" I said, looking for a hidden sword, or knife, or a bow.

"To continue talking, but I'm going to choose the subject. And I want you to answer, even if you don't want to, which is going to take more courage than you've ever been called upon to use."

"You mean we're going to sit here and you're going to yammer at me about—about my father, and the stupidity of *feelings*, until I answer? Why?" I demanded, thoroughly revolted.

"To save you from a long, hard fall. Tell me, how old was your father when he took over in Methden?"

"He was twenty," I snapped.

"In what year?"

"'37!" I ground out the "7" with superlative sarcasm.

"What happened to your grandfather, and why?"

"He wouldn't give up his plans to conquer the coast, which the Regent had agreed to. He lied to the new king about some executions, um—I forget what else. What's the purpose of this questioning about the past? It's over!"

"And? After the king routed him and sentenced him to exile, your grandfather did what?"

"Went south. Became a mercenary. Died tangling with a real vicious gang of thieves somewhere in The Bridge."

"Your father's reaction, as told to you later?"

I shrugged in the darkness, ignoring the tensing of my stomach. "He'd always hated him. Thought he'd betrayed his vows. Got exactly what he deserved. So?"

"Your father married when?"

"'42."

"Why?"

"*What?*"

"*Why*—he's told you, why?"

"Oh, what idiocy! Have you been drinking, or are you just demented? He said he married her because he"—I whined this sarcastically—"fell in love." I made a juicy and realistic gagging noise.

"Why?"

"Oh, *will* you—"

"What's the matter, afraid of the words?"

"Just as afraid as I am of butterflies! He said she was 'showing him a side of life like spring after a very long winter.' *What* meaningless rat shit. So he had a soft side, do you condemn him for that?"

"On the contrary! I praise him for it. But I wanted you to acknowledge that he had this other side, and that your molding yourself into a caricature of his military side was for a reason. Now! When did your father first turn from you to direct Ret's raising, talking about his training for the academy, for possible heirship, leaving your education to your mother?"

"He didn't 'turn away,' he just—"

"Oh, yes he did. And then he gave up on Retren and came back to you after you had kept the house in turmoil trying to regain his attention. But all you got was beatings. And did he say anything to you afterward?"

"Just to ask if I was going to do whatever it was again..." I said slowly, then added firmly, "And if I would, I said yes! I never lied to him!"

"Did he praise you for that?"

"Yes. Said I'd been born with his nature, and it was an irony Ret was born with Mother's."

"That was about the time he gave up on tutoring Retren, and left him to you. To which you responded with your determination to become better than the best. Why did you have to be better than the best?"

"I told you, he said if I went to the academy I'd be bullied and that would ruin Methden's rep, and I agreed."

"Yet girls had been allowed to join the army ever since the compulsory attendance rules for jarls' sons were changed. Did you know that the girls who came were scoring high in their years?"

"Of course," I scoffed. "Father said that any girl who wanted in had to be the *best.*"

"You mean better than the average boy?"

"Yes!"

"Why?"

"Because Methden had pride in its —"

"Because girls weren't as good as boys. So 'the best girl' was only equal to an average boy. And that meant *you.*"

"That's not true!"

"And you strove and strove to become the most militant teen in Methden's history, but all along you knew you would always be second-rate in his eyes because you were a girl, and it was only Retren's having failed more by being a dreamer that put you back in his attention. And you were glad to keep Retren out of your father's eye there, lest he replace you again."

"Shi —"

"*You believed it so thoroughly* that when Ramond Vendren, a big, healthy son of one of Methden's wealthiest and most revered citizens, who wanted to go outside the country to study art, out of anger borne of envy told you that you wouldn't be sent to the academy because you were a little girl, you never even questioned what made him strike out at you that way. The fathers knew, though, and each for his own reasons tacitly allowed you to humiliate Ramond again and again, for years. He was to be toughened and stung out of what was considered a suitable career for girls and to embrace the honorable art of war. An attitude absolutely rife in this country." He sighed, rubbing his eyes with two fingers. "We're still not far removed from the empire-conquerors." Almost under his breath, "And changing that's going to be the wrench of the century."

The blackness and anger had long since clouded my brain, making it impossible for me to get up and run away. I hugged my knees up tight against me, my arms locked hard around them, tighter, tighter, but I could not contain the boiling, acid anger roiling and burning and clawing me from the inside.

Van gave a short sigh. "Let's finish. So the binding emotion you've had all your life was the conviction you had disappointed your father at birth. You never wanted to *be* a boy, which would have been easy enough to fix—"

"Easy," I scoffed, the bitterness welling up. "The healers could put me through pain so my body would change, but they said that they could not guarantee what I wanted, which was height. Strength. All changing my sex would get me would be my becoming the tiniest man in Marloven history. And the biggest joke."

Van went on as if I hadn't spoken. "What you wanted was what you thought boys had. Your father's love for you was at best conditional, and came out expressed only in approval when you two succeeded in a deed he deemed worthy of his own high standards for himself. You, second-rate as a daughter, and Retren, second-rate as a son because he had a hankering for the beauty in words. Think of him! Beaten for daydreaming—termed laziness—his education abandoned in disgust by a father who robbed your mother of any efficacy she might have had for you both by indicating *her* education was only worthy of foreigners. There's Retren, seven or eight years old, and to prove to your father you can be a leader you give him attention, fun, a reason to live! Everything he did was for you. He knew he was worthless in your father's eyes, and he was ashamed of his comforting visits to your mother. The best he could ever hope for was to be your lieutenant, and your occasional words of praise warmed him exactly like your father's warmed you."

I wanted more badly than I had wanted anything in my life to argue. But I couldn't. It was so clear. There we were, Da trying to see me as good as a boy. Retren trying to see himself as good as I was. Imry Llyenthur walks in and sees us all. "You were half one of us all along," he'd said to me.

I was the weakest, not the strongest. I was the one who listened to him, who followed along, betraying everything I'd ever been taught because he said he'd make me a commander. Like my father had almost promised.

But first, I had to sacrifice Retren in the ultimate betrayal.

Retren.

Imry Llyenthur had not done it, or that distant, horrible Svirle of Yssel, but *I*. I had nearly made Ret pay with his life for his stubbornly held convictions, for his nature, for being a boy with free access to everything I wanted and he didn't. It was *I* who nearly murdered him, just as if I'd rushed him with a knife in my hand.

In order to get a command that was probably as fake as any lighter symbol Imry had scorned.

"Oh, you would have clawed your way to the top for real," Van said. "You forgot your mind-shield. Your thoughts are screaming even if you aren't. You would have clawed your way up, one bloody corpse at a time. Beginning with your own people if they dared to stand against you, and then you probably would have turned on Imry Llyenthur, if he didn't gut you first. Because that is how promotion works in Norsunder. Or maybe you would waken one day, and feel remorse, and wonder how you got there, hated by everyone around you. Maybe you might even regret some of your actions. But Retren, who above anyone else had been most faithful to you, would. Still. Be. Dead."

Nausea twisted my insides right to the heart—and the grief I had been fighting against all this time broke the inner wall. Not the mind-shield. That was still there, imperfect as it was. The much higher, older wall I'd built my shield against, me on one side and emotions on the other.

I laid my face on my knees, my teeth clenched so hard my jaw ached, and for the first time since I was scorned and slapped out of it when I was very small, I wept. I'd despised the weakness of tears, as Father had. I had not shed a single tear after the news about father dying in battle, and I'd been proud of my inner strength of will, wishing he could see me dry-eyed and bent on vengeance.

But I sure opened the floodgates now.

Van didn't cravenly creep away, though I'm sure he heard my gulps and shudders and no doubt wished himself anywhere else.

When they had subsided a little, he said, "Rage and grief are two of the strongest emotions we have. And I know very well that we Marlovens are taught from the cradle that rage, at least, can be shaped into a tool. For revenge. For justice, which sometimes is merely another name for revenge. Whereas grief leaves us with nothing." His voice husked on the last word. "But there is another perspective that I invite you to consider. Which is, rage too frequently costs lives. Grief doesn't. That's it for the lessons. Want company?"

I was beyond speaking, but he successfully interpreted my twitch of a shoulder as a No. I didn't hear him leave, I just know after about ten infinities I looked up, hiccoughing, surprised it was still dark. My body ached, especially my ribs, but inside I felt empty, clear down to the insides of my toes.

I looked around. Even the horses were gone, though Van had left a field bedroll. I was too empty to unroll it properly and crawl in. I flung it over me right there on the grass, and stared up at the stars through the faintly rustling budding branches, and almost immediately fell asleep. And then I cried in my dreams.

Sixteen

THE RHYTHMIC DRUM OF horse hooves woke me.

In dawn's faint blue light Van walked toward me, leading both horses. His head was down. When he was near, he looked up and said, "We'd best head back. The farm'll be up and about soon."

I got slowly to my feet, my head hammering in time with my heartbeat.

"What happens," I said hoarsely, "when the Norsundrians are once again able to come and go between Norsunder and our world? If we kill them will they just come back?"

He said, "How Norsunder works is complicated, and I don't completely understand it. I do know that they can consent to a bloodknife spell, which enables them to maintain a life, but I believe they lose much of themselves in that bargain. And they can be entirely subsumed into the center of Norsunder, to be used at the whim of those who've the power to tap the center."

I heaved myself onto the horse. After a time, I said, "Forever?"

"That I can't tell you. I expect there's always hope, but what hope means in Norsunder I don't know."

I don't remember any of the ride back, except the perceptible lightening of the sky above. Only the brightest stars were left, glimmering weakly in the west, when we reached the pottery farm.

Miraculously, no one was in the stable. We dismounted and began unsaddling and grooming the horses, but my hands were slow, and a task I knew well was almost beyond me. Abruptly a hand lifted the brush from mine; Van said, "I'll finish. Go on in and get some shut-eye."

Miraculously no one was around in the yard, or the long hall. I was soon asleep.

And was tortured by dreams. Vivid ones, mostly of Retren. Finally I woke up when the door closed. A tray of fast-cooling food had been set on the table.

I got up, and ate. All the time I kept thinking in my old mode, and yet outside of it, a weird expansion of consciousness and awareness that rendered every tiny sound—the unseen birds, the chuckle of the stream, the occasional distant hail from someone working out in the clay-beds—every sight—the dents in the legs of the little table, the peeling whitewash on the stone walls, the angle of the sunlight lancing down to the floor—preternaturally clear, so clear they were nearly unbearable.

I ran my fingers back and forth over the weave of the blanket, thinking that it was not touch, or smell, that hurt. It was the absence of anger that left all the more room for the pain of remorse. Of grief.

When I was done eating I passed my hands over my eyes, which were still stinging and gritty from dried tears, and I saw dirt smeared on my wrist. I looked down. The robe was rumpled and grass- and dirt-marked. And beneath it, my underthings, not changed for days.

Just thinking about it turned me into one gigantic itch.

Was I permitted out? I did not remember hearing the bar thump into place.

I stood there the longest time, unable to test to find out. The thought that I might still be a prisoner was so sickening, so overwhelming I could not force my hand to the thick, rough wood of the door.

A rap on the door caused me to jump. Van entered, and behind him Lnand. She shot me a considering look, picked up the dishes, and left.

Van studied my face, and his tense mouth relaxed. "It worked," he said, and dropped into the chair. "Oh, no doubt you'll be snarling at me again. But you know now what your personal enemy is. And how to fight it. It's going to take work," he added. "Probably as difficult as you have ever done."

"I've got to see Retren," I said. "And apologize."

Van tipped his head. "That can happen. But first, I want you to remember that understanding and forgiveness don't necessarily follow neatly one after the other."

"I've got to make it up to him," I said, my stomach tightening against more tears. "*Now.*"

"So-called atonement is a funny thing." He smiled a little. "No sooner is one involved than it turns into an obligation. Then resentment. And so the cycle begins. A joke on human nature," he added, "but I see you're not in a laughing mood. Never mind. You can't go back to your old relationship with your brother. You do get that, right?"

"Right."

"So you go on. For you, today is day one. But that doesn't mean you can expect the same for all the other people in your life. Do you see what I mean?"

"You mean consequences."

"I do. You might find yourself facing a different sort of battle. Every watch. Every day, at first. Not just against the consequences of your actions. Against the habit of hitting out first with that ready anger. That will be tougher than facing others, because habit is so easy to fall back into."

"What do I do now?"

"For now, come out. Help around the farm. Take each person one at a time. Beyond that, we've got to get the kingdom back. Then, you get an education and help rebuild the country."

"Where's Ret?"

"He's feeding the chickens."

"Can I see him?"

"I'll ask," he said.

I'll ask. There was the first thrust of the invisible sword. And it hurt.

"Tdor has been wanting to visit you. Up to it?"

I gave a laugh. It sounded like I was strangling. "I guess."

He went out—leaving the door ajar. I leaned back and shut my eyes.

I'd scarcely taken two breaths before I heard quick steps, and there was Tdor, looking bony and brown, in her usual aproned robe. Her eyes were wide, her braids wispy. "Marend!" She stopped in the doorway, then frowned at the room. "This is so small, how'd you bear it?"

Habit, Van had said. "I ignored it."

She grinned. "I couldn't. I have to see the sky. Whee-ew, do you stink! It smells like a pack of dogs has been burrowed here, and it looks like you've been rolling around in the mud, wearing that thing that would cover a horse. C'mon! They've got a nice bath here. The water's cold, but you won't mind that."

I picked at the folds of dirty fabric. "I don't think I could stand to bathe and put this damn thing back on."

"I have an extra robe. If you can stand it?" she added a little self-consciously.

"It'll still be big." I groaned. "But at least not so much like a tent."

She laughed, and led me down the hall and to a stairway to the basement. "Today the girls get the bath in the morning. It's late—everyone's gone to work. We should have it to ourselves."

The bath was fed by the stream. It was cold, which flashed chill through me, but then felt delicious. They had soap waiting in dishes, which I used to scrub all over. There was a tub beside the pool, with laundry-beating sticks. I hauled myself out of the bath and warmed up by laundering my underthings, and then the hated blue robe.

When I was done, Tdor handed me some worn, neatly mended underthings that smelled like sunshine, and a faded green robe with a plain undyed sash. I suspected that these were her only other clothes. I said, awkwardly and self-consciously, "Thanks." I wrestled into them, sighing when, as usual, they were far too long. But at least the robe hem didn't drag on the ground, as she wore her robes above ankle length.

When we'd dressed and hung out the wet clothes over the racks near the kiln, we walked outside in the sun to dry our hair, I hesitated, then forced the words out, "I feel like a road apple after a horse ate too much bran mash."

"Ah, Van explained how Llyenthur set you up from the start. And that you really didn't rat on our plan and sic the Norsundrians on us."

"Wha—Llyenthur said I did?"

She crossed her arms. "More or less hinted that to Ret and Kelsan and Noll that, when they bagged 'em."

That gave me a sickening wrench. "No. The only thing I told him was that it was my plan, but that was *after* it happened."

She flung up her hands. "Then he twisted the truth. Van said you really weren't in charge of anything, and if you *had* tried to take real command they all would have ignored you, unless you did what he told you to do."

I said, hating every word, "He played me for a fool, and I was a fool to fall for it."

She grinned. "It's such a relief to have *you* back!"

I looked at her skeptically.

"What?" she said, hands on her hips.

"I'm not saying I didn't deserve it, but last time we saw each other, you gave me the back of your hand."

"I did no such thing," she exclaimed indignantly. "I didn't even see you, except as a shadow. I was doing that to that horseapple Norsundrian."

So much, I thought, for all focus being on me. Except that Retren had been staring right at me, I was absolutely sure.

Tdor looked away, then said quickly, "We really need to figure something to do! Oh—we took a vote, you know, and they decided you're welcome back. Otherwise Van said he'd take you away somewhere. Come on, say hi—we *all* had to run away. Even the rats," she added, sidling me an anxious glance.

"Fine!" I said sturdily, thinking *day one*. The old anger had surged up. I had to breathe to fight the resentment. Breathe, breathe. Day one. "I owe Ramond an apology."

"Oh, well, you'll like him, I think. He's a bit squirrely, but the painters here all are squirrely. Come on!"

"How did Ret vote?" I asked.

"I don't know," she said. "Secret ballot." But her eyes were serious as she plopped down at the end of the kitchen garden cabbage bed. "Help me weed? I took this chore because I'm good at it at home."

She had to show me what to do, but weeding is not hard.

After a time I sat back to wipe my hair out of my eyes, and caught Tdor looking my way. A brief grin flashed. "Huh, it's weird to see you in colors, and doing kitchen work! I'm so used to you in black, running with steel."

"You haven't mentioned Ret," I said.

Her smile vanished. "Wasn't sure what to say. He's had nightmares, almost every night."

I sighed, my guts crawling with a new conviction. "*He* burned my clothes. Right?"

She spread her hands. "It was pretty creepy. Noll and Kelsan were fine, mostly, after we freed 'em that night. Ret was quiet. Wouldn't talk to anybody. *We* thought maybe Llyenthur'd put a spell on him but Van said no — Van's got *that* stuff —" She tapped her forehead. "Anyway, Ret just kind of sat around and did what he was told until we came here, and we were all in the kitchens that night, when Lnand and I came in from undressing you and cleaning that horrid cut and putting on the bandage, and Ret saw me carrying your duds, and he suddenly jumped up, and grabbed them, and threw them in the fire, and he — well, he started choking and sobbing, and then Van came running, and took him out, and he started having these nightmares every night, but he's been himself during the day. Quieter. He's never said anything to us about you at all, so I can't tell you how he voted, like I can the rest of us. I mean, *we* talked about our votes, and we all voted for you to stay! That is," she added conscientiously, "if you want to."

I had to get it over with, and I wasn't going to do it cringing in that damned room. "Then show me around!"

"You want to wait a day?" she asked, eyeing me up and down. "Now that I can really see you, you look as terrible as Ret. Your eyes are still salt, and I know I'm scrawny — though Ma promises I'll plump out once I pass sixteen — but you look like one puff of wind would blow you away."

"I haven't been eating much," I said. "Thought it was strength of will."

She yanked viciously at the root of a sprawling weed that was doing its best to choke a cabbage, then sat back on her heels. "Ma said once, that as a jarl, your da was the best there could be. Fair to all in judgment, not just his people. Fierce when it came to bandits marauding over the border.

Tough in training. A great jarl, but he was a terrible father. Though not as bad as his father had been."

I wrinkled my nose. It was strange to think of the adults being our age, and knowing each other.

She duck-waddled to the next row, and started weeding again. "If you stay, you have to do work. We're living with the prenties, but we don't get to do much with the pottery. You can help me, if you like." She laughed. "It's fun here, though I miss Ma, and Methden! But we can't go back."

My fault. She didn't say it. Might not have thought it. But it was true all the same.

Day one. Day one, my mind said, but really, as she chattered, I scanned around, I saw plenty of people coming and going. I was looking for Ret. I did not see him.

When we were done, she took me to the clay area. All the girls were apprentices or journeyworkers. She introduced me, and they either greeted me politely or stared, then went right on talking about things and people I did not know.

I slowly backed away. I really wanted to see Retren. I needed to see him.

Bigger boys and girls lugged crates of pottery to lattice-work sheds. Several rats were among them, none of whom approached me, and Rom walked slowly behind them, absorbed in carrying a tray of fragile cups and trying to smooth his gait.

No Retren. Then Ramond dashed in, hair flying, and stumbled to a stop when he saw me.

I swallowed. "Ramond. I guess I owe you an—"

He flushed with obvious relief, and when he shrugged, he almost upset his tray of cups. "All over! If I'd had any wit I would have left town years ago."

"But for me—"

"Wasn't just you. My da was part of it, cheering you on secretly. Forget it." He turned even redder. "It's almost worth it, to come here. They are letting me paint! Just eagle-claw patterns and running horses, and on mixing bowls and the like, but I'm getting to *paint!*"

He looked at me eagerly, and I understood that he expected me to be excited. "That's great," I said awkwardly.

He carried his cups away and I wandered on, seeking Retren.

I felt his presence before I saw him, and anything else I might have said went out of my head.

Retren stood near the door to one of the buildings, talking to Van. He was very thin, but even so, it seemed that he had grown a little. His hair was rioting wildly over his head just as mine probably was—a haircut was a month overdue.

As I started toward him, he gestured to someone else, smiling in a way I had not seen in a long time, and my heart twisted inside me. When he saw me, the smile vanished, and my heart twisted the rest of the way.

I know how stupid that sounds. Hearts don't leap around and dance inside your ribs, or it would be a whole lot harder to kill enemies. But that is just what it felt like.

He half turned away, and then jammed his hands in his pockets, and waited, clearly braced for nastiness. From me.

I don't even remember crossing the yard. As I got close I saw how thin his face was, how his chin was starting to emerge long and angular. Like Da's. His expression was closed.

When I reached him, I discovered we were eye to eye. His were dark, and wary.

"Marend." His quiet voice was flat.

"Ret. I'm sorry. About everything."

He jerked a shoulder up without speaking.

I rambled on, "I've lost count of the days. But it was your birthday they were celebrating yesterday, wasn't it?"

"Yeah." He shrugged. "Yours is next week."

"I'd just as soon keep it to myself," I said. "Mind not saying anything?"

He shook his head.

Then, habit made me say, "Tell the gang."

His lips compressed. "*You* tell them."

"I will," I said, heartsick again.

His gaze slid away from mine, going distant. I moved aside, and he walked away.

I took a few steps without being aware of it, then Van said next to me, in a conversational tone, "You know he's bound to challenge you."

I swung around. "What do I do?" I tried to hide my stinging eyes, then gave up.

"You're asking *me*? I don't know. I never had a brother. Fight back, sit back and take it, stay neutral. You could even reverse your old roles, which would be thoroughly rotten for you both. Remember, your mistake is behind you. You've just got to prove it." He glanced around, then said more quietly, "I'm going to leave soon, and I think I'll take Ret with me. I want to go around the country. See how things are. And I've got to try to find places for those who're in danger at home."

"Have you told the others?"

"Only Retren, as yet."

I shrugged, a jerky movement, because it hurt so much, that last remote gaze of Retren's.

When the anger had been the worst, I worked out. Maybe that would be the right thing to do for this pain of regret, and sorrow.

I ran back to seek Tdor in the gardens. Father had always said, when trying to make a decision, there was nothing like labor to clear the head. If one had already done enough drilling and scrapping for the day, one ought to look for the most urgent task waiting, and get to it.

Tdor pointed out the girl in charge of their group. "What do I do?" I asked. "Put me to work."

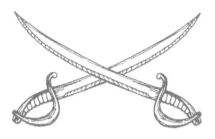

Seventeen

I SPENT THE REST of the morning with Tdor. After lunch we were free, so Tdor took me down to see the masters and select journeyworkers painting the porcelain. I admired their skill, but I was not excited by the patterns of scrollwork, twined leaves, etc. I liked the ones with more familiar motifs, like screaming eagles and running horses. The style I thought looked best of all was dyed a deep, deep cobalt blue, with a thin gold ring painted along the rim of cup and saucer.

Tdor and I admired it, she saying that the local Norsundrian garrison had informed Nalenda that they expected a certain number of items, which would be selected by their quartermaster, but the rest they could sell as before. The journeyworkers debated hotly whether or not to hide the best stuff from them.

At night, after a dinner was served in the basement, at rows of mismatched tables, we helped wash and peel vegetables, and partially mix and knead bread ingredients, for baking the next morning. There was light talk and laughter among the others, but I sensed a little constraint because of my presence. My mind was occupied with Ret, sitting with Van, Sindan, Rom, and one of the rats whose name I did not know. I did not approach Retren; I hoped he would find his way to me. Each time I glimpsed him and he did not come to me hurt worse than the one before.

That night I went back and slept in the storeroom that everyone seemed to regard as mine. I had trouble sleeping. I kept seeing Ret's big dark-gray eyes, wary and distant. I tried—hard—not to let the anger back in, but really, I preferred it to the pain.

Next morning Van appeared at my side as I ran down the stairs to breakfast in the basement. He looked younger—brighter. "Ret slept through the night," he murmured.

A little of the pain eased inside me. I said, "And so did you?"

He sighed. "Enjoyed every moment. Or I would have, if I'd been awake!"

I laughed at this absurdity because he expected me to, though there was no laughter inside me. I was spared having to say anything more by the hordes of hungry people pushing between us.

Lnand sat down with the youngest girl prenties, all about ten—the same age as those chosen to go to the academy. When I caught her eye, she gave me a quizzical look, and a kind of smile.

The little girls all stared at me as I came up to her. My heartbeat thudded in my ears. "I want to apologize for the trouble I caused you," I said.

She lifted her hand. "It's all right."

Tdor called, "Here, Marend!"

I turned away gratefully, and plunked down onto the plain bench next to Tdor, where I could see Ret sitting with Rom and Sindan, the latter turning his head back and forth so he could see me, and everyone else.

Tdor thumped the table, making the dishes rattle. "In two days, we'll be stuck with laundry. It's grim, working late at night while people sleep, then early morning going to the kiln to gather the dry things, because so few have second clothes, and we couldn't risk buying local and causing questions about why there are so many new apprentices, when it's usually a handful. But once it goes through the press, we're free for the rest of the day!"

Despite the warnings, I found laundry no more or less toilsome than any other chore. Harder was the long watch of freedom. I did my best to mix in with the group, but I could see in sudden self-consciousness and changed conversations that I was still an outsider, even if they weren't talking about me.

I spent a lot of my free time alone, drilling, then remaking that overlarge robe. I asked permission. It turned out it was left from someone who had died in the fighting, and it went unclaimed. I cut it up and made it into a long tunic and riding trousers. With every stitch, I brooded. I wanted badly to right myself in the eyes of the world…in my own eyes…well, in Ret's.

Once I had the new clothes done, I laundered Tdor's, gave them back, and then ventured out again. I tried twice to approach Ret, but each time he greeted me, and drifted away after very little was said.

Then, three days later, rainclouds tumbled in on a cold wind. I climbed to the roof to let the strengthening breeze blow in my face. The pain came and went like the sea tides are said to do, leaving numbness. Emptiness. I had no purpose.

And then I heard his voice.

"Marend. Did you remember it's your birthday to-day?"

I turned. Hadn't heard him approach. "I did this morning." I looked down at myself. "Fifteen. And I still look like I'm six."

Ret's eyes gleamed silvery as he grinned. "*I* don't have to grow up. Yet. If I don't want. He said I ought to spend some time the age I am now to catch up with myself. I don't know what that means, exactly. But it sounds like fun, especially as he promised I don't ever have to go to the academy if I don't want to." He paused, and neither of us moved, but there, in the air, was an invisible slap. He even flinched a little, though he had never flinched when either Da or I hit him.

Then he shook his overlong hair back. "Maybe he can do the spell for you too."

"*What*? What spell? What is it like? Is Van a mage?" Somehow it was easy to believe he knew magic.

"He can't do it until the dark-magic spell is lifted here, or until we get out of the country, to some place where light-magic works. How I'd love to travel — and we might!"

Ret's face lifted with pleasure.

I had no more desire to protract being underage and undersized any more than I desired to leave the country, but I said only, "I want to go to the academy."

Retren transferred his gaze to my face. "Tell him, before we go. You knew we were going to go away?"

"Van told me he was taking you around the kingdom. But what can he do about it? Even if he's a mage, it's still the king, and the Headmaster, who decide those things. That is, if Norsunder wasn't here."

Retren studied me, then said, "He told me we'll leave on Sixthday if the rain holds, and travel under cover of it." He sounded pleased. Then, "Since there's no academy now. What are you going to do?"

"I don't know. I got an idea, though." I looked east again, and scanned the dark forest-line. "I don't want to stay here. I want to get back at the Norsundrians. I thought—just before you came—of maybe riding to that forest. See if maybe I could set up some sort of hideout. Van said he's going to need a place to send refugees. It might be impossible, though. But it's something, the only idea I've had."

"It sounds good," Ret said cautiously. "But wouldn't the Norsundrians find houses? and what about food?"

"We'd dig underground. The idea came to me at breakfast, when I was looking around their basement. One can hide a lot underground. Food? I don't know. Maybe I can ask Van." It seemed natural to ask him.

"You can ask him now, if you want." Retren said.

"I don't know where he is."

"I can call him." Ret's upper lip lifted in triumph. Or maybe glee—there's often malice in triumph, and there wasn't any in my brother. "Watch." He shut his eyes for a heartbeat or two, then looked up at me.

Half a small glass later Van topped the stairs and strode rapidly toward us, smiling. "What is it, scrub?"

Retren received this insult with obvious pleasure. "She's got an idea."

"Let's hear it." Van hunkered down near us.

I explained my thoughts. He listened, pursed his lips, and then clapped his hands on his knees. "You're right, getting food might be tough, particularly in winter. But not impossible. You really want to try it?" He studied me.

I assented firmly

Van faced the east meditatively.

I said, "Wouldn't Darchelde be a good headquarters? No one goes there as a rule."

"It would," he said. "But a lot of work, building. Staying undetected, particularly if they start searching. Darchelde is a funny forest. The eastern half is still recovering from a bad magic-blasting many years ago, but the west...you might just find the trees, and the life there cooperating."

"*What*? Trees?"

"They're alive, aren't they? I've been told, many times, of forest dwellers whose footfalls are soundless, and whose faces are never scratched by twigs while being chased by skilled Norsundrian hunters who nevertheless trip over vines they didn't see, crack twigs, and so forth. You would have to cooperate with the forest life. And I repeat, it would be a lot of work, fashioning something that wouldn't be detected."

"I'm not afraid of work."

"Great. How 'bout if we ride out tomorrow and take a look, if the rain's not too bad?"

"Oh, yes!" I said with enthusiasm. "What, the three of us?"

"Couple more, if they like the idea. I'll set it up."

"What about chores?"

"I'll fix that, too. After all, if we're leaving soon they'll be closing ranks anyway."

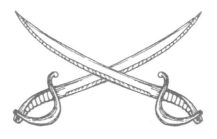

Eighteen

SO IT WAS.

That not-quite-numb sense of emptiness started lifting early the next morning. I slept well, and I woke up restless, but not with anger. It was a lighter sense, more like purpose and possibility.

Van and Retren were at the stable when I showed up. With them were Ramond and one of the older girls who had been an academy second-year named Cam, tall with pale blond hair in a long braid that bounced on her horse's back. She had big hands, and strong-looking arms. Betting myself she was hot stuff with a sword (and that it had come easy) I fought against envy. She had bright blue eyes, and smiled at me when I came in. I forced down the envy as I lent a hand with the last of the saddling, and we rode out in the drizzling dawn.

I had learned stealth in the city. Now I got a lesson in stealth cross country. Cam, short for Camdan, led us eastward in a meandering route across fields and a couple streams, always sticking to low ground where tracks were least likely to last, if we could not avoid them altogether, and always single file. We seldom saw a house and never a town. Only once did we hide behind a hedgerow, and it turned out to be for a hay wagon.

"Still, might be bound for Norsundrian stables," Van said. "Best be safe by being cautious."

We entered a gently rolling shrubland just before noon, and shortly after that were swallowed by the forest. It was old. There was a lot of oak, and other twisted and spreading trees I didn't know the names of. The air, even with the rain, smelled different — lingered refreshingly in the lungs.

We rode for a time, then Ramond spoke. "Here. South, now. Not too far from that stream — and not too close, or you'll get wet ground."

I'd thought the silence was the others considering whether it was possible. Now Ramond talked as though it was settled.

"What're you looking for?" I asked.

"Ground that does some of the work for us. Always near water, not just for drinking, but there's usually hollows or fissures or the like." He grinned at my face. "I learned something about it when my Da went through a short phase of trying to sidetrack me into building by letting me study architecture. You have to know ground to build well."

I looked skeptically at the mossy, rough ground.

"Rocky terrain like this will also help disguise the entrance," Van said. "But we'll have to make sure coming and going is done over rocks. Trails are worn faster than you think, in which case you may as well put up a plinth with a carving, **Secret Cave Here** —>

Ramond jerked his hair back, then laughed. "Take a vote of the others to see who's willing to work on it, but I can guess it'll be unanimous."

Cam raised her hand. "I'll sound out some of the locals; I know most of 'em. So many are burning for justice after the Pass."

A brief silence heightened tension at that mention, with shifted glances.

"We could get a start on gathering supplies," she said hastily.

"You'd join us?" I asked.

She smiled. "No. I have to help at the pottery until we get the academy back. I'll pass messages. Arrange supplies. And I'll dig."

Retren stared reflectively up through the tree-branches. Van looked around in satisfaction.

We found a huge, spreading tree that formed a ceiling overhead. There we halted and ate a lunch of wrapped sandwiches. After a little talk about getting started on the hideout, we left for the long ride back.

Half a glass after we returned, Van and Ramond and I called a meeting of all the Methden folk. Van presented the plan—or began to. Once they got the gist of it, they drowned out his words with yips and cheers. Everyone was restless, not just me. Well, it figures, since they joined gangs in the first place.

They gabbled their own ideas, not listening to anyone else's. Van sat back, smiling, and let them do it, so I slipped out.

And found Retren at the top of the stairs, reading a book by the torch on the wall. I hadn't noticed him leaving.

He put his book down. "I knew they'd go for it."

I agreed. "Half of it's Van. What an example of the opposite type of leadership than Llyenthur's! Although, looking at it coldly, I imagine one gets more loyalty, more trustworthy followers, when they come to you of their own free will—" I stopped my ruminations because Retren was biting his lip, trying not to smile. "Did I say something funny?"

He shook his head, then put his book under his arm and scrambled to his feet. "Come on. Let's go outside."

We stood under the awning and watched rain drizzling into the muddy yard. Raindrops caught light from the torch behind us, seemed to burn briefly before disappearing.

"He said I could tell you if I wanted to, but to keep it to yourself. He's the king."

I took in a sharp breath. *"Senrid-Harvaldar?* No."

"No?" Ret's entire face lit with mirth.

"He's too short."

Now Retren was openly laughing at me, though without any sound.

As the truth began to assert itself, I said hastily, "Not that he's *short* short. Like me. Not short at all—I think he's taller than Sereth. It's just that I always imagined the king to be this great figure, bigger than Cam. Bigger than anyone. Da always said he had a king's presence. I thought that meant he was taller than anyone else. Don't tell him I said he's short."

"He wouldn't care," Retren said with an assurance that amazed me.

I was about to exclaim that Van being Senrid-Harvaldar was impossible, but then I thought back, and back. Small things began to add up, mostly having to do with how well he knew the royal city. How he had spoken as if very familiar with Father.

I turned to Retren. "*You* knew."

He compressed his lips, eyes narrow and wary.

"Since — ?"

"Pretty much from the beginning."

"Wow." I let out a long breath this time. "So Mother was right."

"Yes," he said softly. "He *did* come back."

I hadn't thought much about her, and now I winced. "What does she know?"

"The king visited her the day when — " There was the slightest pause in his voice. " — the execution was planned. He said you were skulking around in our part of the castle, lost in your own nightmare. He told Ma the plan, and that if she heard nothing, she'd know it was successful. If not, Llyenthur'd be in to gloat."

"She knows we're here?"

"No, but she knows the king has us."

"The king." My mind flickered from Mother's face in memory to his in the present. "It figures. How'd he find — oh. His mind stuff?"

"Yes. It was the day we got caught. He was walking the streets of Methden, checking things out, and he got the mess from Sindan, who was out doing deliveries. Followed him, talked to him, Sindan took him to Tdor, who took him to Ramond. Then he made the plan to free us, and get you."

I shuddered, remembering that night. A bubble of nausea surged up from my guts. "Retren. I really am so sorry, I can't tell you how sick…" My throat tightened, and all the bad feelings boiled up, leaving me unable to speak.

Retren said nothing, and as the stream rushed by below us, there stretched about the most painful silence of my life.

Then there was a step behind us, and *he* appeared. As soon as he saw my face he said with a wry smile at Ret, "You decided to tell Marend?"

Retren spread his hands. "You said I could." But his eyelids lifted in question.

"Sure. I just don't want it generally known until we leave. That much time'll have us exiting from high spirits. More time would give a chance for other less desirable things." I was going to protest, but he forestalled me with a raised hand. "Embarrassment from some for having spoken freely, deference questions, possibly resentment toward Marend when your own rank is remembered. And inevitably talk, which might be overheard."

I looked out toward the rain, overwhelmed with so many reactions. First and strongest, regret. And a sense of unreality, but beneath that the sick conviction that all was real, and I the cause. As always when I'm overwhelmed, my mind reaches for the little things that don't matter. "Van's usually short for Indevan. It's so common!"

"Indevan was the old king's name," Retren said. "You know that! Before the Regent."

"My second name, too. But I've only used it when I'm traveling around the country and don't want to be known."

Belatedly came the important things. "Van—Senrid-Harvaldar, I am so sorry about the little princess—"

He turned away sharply, then back, every line of him tight with grief. It shocked me. My mouth flapped like a carp's as I tried to think of something mitigating to say, but how do you mitigate anguish?

"Let's go inside," he said abruptly, and hopped to the wall and down.

Retren and I followed. We walked across the yard to the long building that housed the boys, or most of them. The stairs took us down to a small room with three wood-paneled and a big castle painted on the stone of the fourth. The king lit a lamp as he said, "Have a seat." He was his old, bland self again.

Retren and I dropped down onto one of the narrow bunks, and wiped rain off our faces, my fingers trembling as the enormity of what I had just learned ringing through my skull.

The king sat across from us, fists on his knees. And when he spoke, it was not about the little princess whom none of us had met. "Don't waste your time worrying about recriminations, or worse, thinking you deserve it.

Why do you think I bored on about all my own past mistakes? And, you want to hear something worse?" His brows rose and his mouth curved sarcastically. "Not ancient, either, recent."

Retren and I sat like two stones. Ret's eyes had narrowed, the color that stormy dark gray.

"I too spent some time in Llyenthur's hands. Did I tell you that? No? And I know the road you trod." He opened his hand toward me.

I said, "You mean he fed your vanity, and *you* fell for it?"

The king grinned. "Nope. Quite the opposite."

"Huh?"

"His approach with me was humiliation, making a mockery of me. My reign. My daughter. Who he killed, by the way." His hand made a sharp motion—a knife strike.

I didn't think it was possible to be more shocked, but I was. Shocked witless.

"Then he offered me reports on what he was doing here. It didn't matter if I believed what was written or not. The fact that he offered was a constant reminder that I was helpless to do anything about it. He could torch the kingdom and I could do nothing. Added to that, he was in and out during all watches, between my sessions with his bully boys, so I never got much sleep. I had to ask for meals, and then he insisted on eating with me while he talked on and on about what he planned to do with the kingdom, assuming I'd be aiding him. It was excruciating, and though I didn't hop the fence, if I was still there after all this time, who knows what anger would have driven me to?"

"How did you escape?" I asked.

"I was rescued."

"But you would have escaped!"

"Maybe. More likely I would have died trying. Don't know. Didn't happen. My point here is that I endured all the anger and frustration he wanted me to endure, and things could have gone very bad indeed for Marloven Hess, all because of my stupidity in getting caught. Should I toss myself in the dungeon for that stupidity, once we rid ourselves of Norsunder?"

"Of course not," Ret scoffed. "You have to be the king

again. Too many people count on you!"

"Exactly. My responsibilities do not end, they increase. I not only need to do my duties the right way, I have to make reparations for my errors. And I will. But first there is a war to win. We all have weaknesses, and it's Llyenthur's practice—and pleasure—to exploit those. Your first responsibility is to stay out of his hands, and incidentally cheat him out of some fun." A brief, pained smile.

"He did have fun," I said morosely. "He was laughing *at* me. Not with me. I wish I'd seen it then."

"Second, to start educating yourselves, even while we prepare to win the country back, so we can start rebuilding right away. Marloven Hess is full of people like you and me, Marend—and like your father was—who accept most of the lighter precepts, but who still cling to the old ways. A country whose most honorable occupation is moving up the ranks in the army is spending all its talent and energy on one thing, preparation for war. Not defense. There's a difference, though we don't like to see it. Preparation for war is a waste unless you use it, and if you use it, it's destruction. Do you see that?"

The swift flow of words passed me. I managed to pick out the one thing that pertained to me. "You mean, there will be no more academy?"

"No, no, no, I'd have a revolution on my hands, I suspect, if I did that. Though the academy has come and gone over the years. And changed. We'll continue to have it, but it's going to change again, to a focus on defense."

I said morosely, "But I'm fifteen—now I'm too old. And what if it takes ten years to get the kingdom back?"

"If it takes ten years, it takes ten years. And you'll be fighting the entire time, won't you? If at the end of those ten years I call you back to the academy, it would probably be as an instructor in stealth attacks."

In spite of everything, a very small bloom of laughter, and of hope, eased the gaping misery inside me.

He went on, "If it doesn't take that long, the age limits will be negotiable. But first we must win the war."

"Win the war," I repeated, fired to strive with every nerve and wit to make that happen the sooner.

"Meanwhile, I—uh oh." He grimaced.

"Someone overheard us?" Ret pointed at me, then

himself.

The king opened a hand. "One of the little runners. Seems to have been unable to resist being the bearer of Big News. Marend, keep this in mind when discussing Darchelde plans from now on: all it takes is one pair of ears. Right now only the Methden gangs, Cam, and Nalenda know about the Darchelde plan."

"I'll tell Ramond."

"Or I will. I'd better go up and salvage the situation."

"I'll come with you!" Retren said, jumping up.

I could tell Retren was starting to feel about the king the way I had about my father.

I went to my room. I was tired, and I had lots to think about. I knew pretty much what would happen with the others—excitement, loud jabbering, and he'd have to calm them down before talking to them. And I already knew the gist of whatever he'd say.

I poured my tired body into bed. A very strange beginning to being fifteen!

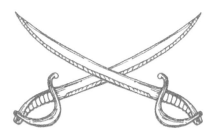

Nineteen

IT SEEMED I'D SCARCELY shut my eyes when an impatient rap at my door startled me into wakefulness. I sat up as Tdor banged in. "Marend! Did you know?"

I just up in bed, and she plumped down at the foot of it. I couldn't see her face, but I could hear her shivering with excitement. "It was wonderful," she said, sighing.

"What's wonderful? That Van is the king?"

"Yes, but he did the sword dance!"

"He *did*?" I wished I'd been there for *that*. "Whose swords did he use? Oh. No one here is armed."

"They found swords," she said quickly. "And hand drums."

"Alone?"

"Oh, no! He tried to beg off at first. Everyone was all excited, and you know how Ramond gets, he was practice-ally dancing without any swords or drums. Then Retren said he'd like very much to see it. All right, said the king, but you know, I don't think he liked it much. Or maybe he was just concentrating on his steps. I don't know, but he said that everybody who knows it could join, even though there were not enough swords. He said knives would do just as well, and you know what? They did! Ramond slam-med his down, but it was the king and Cam who looked the best. Ramond was having fun, you could see it, but he looked like a flapping scarecrow. The rest of us did the drumming, including Retren, and at the end, just now, Ret said to Sindan that Ramond was jumping, and Cam was dancing, but the king made a promise."

I could see it so clearly.

"So," she finished. "What could be a better start to our resistance?"

"What indeed," I said, and because this is a confession, I have to admit that my resolve was already being tested. I was not excited. I was angry, for my first thought was that Ramond had done a splendid job of starting things off as if he'd been the only leader. But I *knew* he probably would not have thought of that. He would jump up and dance because the king was there, and it would be exciting, and anyway, Cam, who was an academy vet, was a better leader than any of us. And Ramond knew it.

As soon as I thought that, I could feel the hot anger dying down. I waited, but no doubts boiled up.

"Marend?" Tdor said. "Are you mad we didn't come get you?"

I almost jumped—I'd actually forgotten she was there.

I took a deep breath and admitted what I'd been thinking.

Tdor's mouth rounded, and she uttered a squawking laugh. Back rushed the hot rage, but she waved her hands. "Oh, Marend, the thought of Ramond trying to oust you...oh, ha ha! Did you know that their plans were all figured out in group? Mostly by Keth, Sindan says. Ramond keeps them all together because they all like him."

I sighed, rubbing my eyes. "I don't even know why it's so important to be in command," I admitted.

"Because your ideas are the best. And you are the fastest. You were the strongest, though now that Rom is getting some size on him—ah, that doesn't matter. Marend, you can't be giving up on us when we're going to be sneaking into creepy Darchelde to commence all that digging. I do NOT look forward to *that*. And how I detest mud!"

"We probably won't start the heavy digging until we know the spring rains are over," I said absently, my mind still on other things. "Before I fell asleep, I was thinking about my parents. Recollecting things. When I was small, smaller than Lesra even. What the king had said was true. My Da valued and respected my mother..." Loved her, but *love* was still one of those words I could not really comprehend. "...and it seems to me that though Mother could buy whatever she wanted, and he would always tell her how beautiful those fancy rugs were, when he wasn't around her, little things he said and did made it clear he thought all those things were foreign foolery. Fuss. Not important, compared to the vital importance of Methden guarding the border and overseeing justice."

Tdor turned her palm up in agreement.

"Do you think my mother knew?"

"She had to, didn't she?" Tdor said. "My ma once said she felt a bit sorry for her, coming from a court to live among us barbarians."

My brooding thoughts were racing on. "And all those horrible lessons, she knew Da wouldn't make me heir, if Retren shaped up. Maybe she thought she was giving me a different life. But I'm too much like Da. How I would hate it!"

"But *she* didn't," Tdor said with her usual practicality. "I'll wager you three laundry days her memories of that stuff are all fond ones."

"And she tried to get me to like it?" I sighed. "Like telling a rock it really ought to be a tree."

"Maybe. But you know, Marend, all this speculation, you could try asking your mother what she thought. When we get back to Methden, of course." She was taken by a sudden yawn. "Talk to her. She's never been mean, not from what everyone says."

The mean one was me. I flinched inside as Tdor yawned again. "What a long day!"

She left.

There was a weird atmosphere when I entered the basement for breakfast. Exhilarated, yet tense. After breakfast, I noticed lots of tight knots of people conversing.

I didn't try to snout my way into any of those groups, but left to take a perimeter ride. I was still sorting things out in my own head.

I had lost the wish to talk to Van since I knew he was the king. Not that I suddenly disliked or was afraid of him — not so — but I suddenly saw him as... it's hard to explain the inward change. During all the foregoing I hadn't really

questioned his origins much. He'd just seemed like someone who had appeared to help. Now that I knew he was
the king, I felt that every word I said might be held against
me as da's heir. At the same time, I also felt that cornering
him for more long confidential talks seemed inappropriate.

I returned in time for the midday meal. In the basement, one look would tell an outsider that the table in the
far corner was the focus of interest. Everyone sat more or
less with their friends, as usual, and as usual there was a
hum of conversation. But looks were shot toward where
Ramond and Cam sat with Retren and the king, head-bent
in earnest conversation.

They glanced my way when I was halfway down the
stairs, and Ramond beckoned. As always, I sought Retren.
There was a faint flush (emotion, not illness) in his thin
cheeks.

"Where were you?" Ramond jabbed his long paint-
stained finger toward a plate. "Saved you some grub.
Making plans for our Resistance!" He squeezed over to
make room.

Ramond was full of ideas, which came very fast. At
first I tried to think of one to each of his but I could not.
Then I noticed some of his ideas were terrible, and *then* I
realized he never seemed to think the consequences
through. The good ones with some possibility were the
same to him as the terrible ones. Tdor and Sindan were
right—it had to be Kethadrend who put a halt to the bad
ideas back when we were all scrapping in Methden.

I won't list any of it down because we discarded most
of it except the fact that the king wanted us to learn the
Norsundrian courier system for the *entire* kingdom. He
said even if they never began sending vital information this
way (and as long as Llyenthur and magic were around,
they wouldn't) it would tell us a lot about their movement
patterns. And when we finally acted, if we nailed all the
vital spots at once, the effect would be devastating—and
we could manage it without having an entire army at our
disposal.

There was a sense of finality about this discussion,
which I finally attributed to the plans the king had made to
leave the next morning.

They were really going! Somehow, I had not believed

it. My sense of well-being immediately dissolved as I watched Retren, and found no echo of my own feeling in his expression.

Yet again, the old acid fire stirred. I struggled to master it, though impatiently. No one hated good emotions. Why must I be continually tortured with bad?

There was still a wall between Retren and me. I could feel it. Was it possible to scale it before he left? What was it Van had said about him—he had a hankering for the "beauty in words." What a meaningless phrase. What *could* it mean? Beauty meant beauty, no other words did, and beauty meant—?

I thought of my mother. I'd heard often how beautiful she was. It had meant soft and silly to me. Then one day, a visiting relation of mother's had told me, with a kind of smirk that raised my hackles, that I must learn to manage my robes better, or my beauty would be wasted. How revolted I was—I had sought a mirror as soon as I could. Had I suddenly changed into a limp, golden-haired decoration? What I saw in the mirror were her gray eyes, and her oval face, but I was reassured by seeing black curls and brown skin like Da's. I took care to avoid that aunt for the rest of her visit, but it had eaten at me until I finally blurted accusingly at my father, "What makes me beautiful and Retren not? *He's* got Mother's eyes too, *and* her pale skin!"

He laughed. "Who told you he wasn't? All of us are; we're a very beautiful family!"

The "we" and his disinterest had reassured me, so I forgot the matter. Besides, why listen to a foolish old aunt anyway? Beauty was obviously one of those *polite* words. Meaningless!

Now I tried to find a meaning for beauty in words, but could not. Retren did, though, or why would the king say so?

And tomorrow Retren would be gone.

Why?

Because there was one aspect in which the king had skirted the truth. Retren was the person I had hurt the most, not me. And it was equally obvious the king thought he'd recover best if removed from my presence.

I became aware again of he sounds of the company finishing lunch, Ramond illustrating some point by waving his knife in the air, and Cam drawing on the table after dipping her finger in her water cup. That sense of loss intensified at the prospect of losing Retren before we could get back to how we were.

Ramond hooted at his own joke, hair hanging in his eyes. Retren grinned at him as he spread honey lavishly on a thick slice of bread. The king—was watching me reflectively. Pride steadied me at once, and self-command reasserted itself.

"Don't you think, Marend?" Ramond turned to me.

"Yes," I said, not knowing what I was agreeing to.

Cam shook her head as she rubbed her nose. "I don't care what you say. Digging could afford the diggers all *kinds* of magical powers much less benefits, and I *still* won't do it, I'm not going to ruin my hands!"

Ramond laughed, echoed by Retren. It was almost like the happy laugh he'd had as a little boy, a laugh I had not heard for a long time.

Retren was happy to be leaving.

No. Retren was happy to be leaving *me*.

Twenty

THE AFTERNOON PASSED IN planning sessions in odd corners, and lots of whispering because no one wanted to be overheard. It caused some resentment among the pottery farm folk. The king was left to smooth it over, but he asked Ramond and me to have the group be a little less public with their private conversations.

There was no problem between Ramond and me. It was odd how we both strongly felt the king should give his approval to the various facets of our plan; he was exactly the person he had been when he introduced me to cutting paper warriors, right down to his borrowed potter's clothes, and yet he wasn't the same person. How much of an aura is solely in the perceiver's eye?

Anyway, Ramond and I went around spreading the word to any Methden people we saw, at which time I saw that Nollard and a couple of the other rats did not want to take orders from me.

When I saw Ramond next, I mentioned it, thinking they were still holding my night in the tower against me. "There's going to be bad feeling unless either they change—or I leave."

His answer surprised me. "Oh, no, that's not it at all! I thought it was all settled. I'm afraid they think you're going to be a tyrant. You've always been so serious, and so *tough!*" He shrugged apologetically. "Make 'em laugh a few times, and—if you don't mind a suggestion—"

"Go ahead."

"Don't go on about discipline. If it turns out we need

it, let's do it gradually, and see if we can convince 'em to vote on it."

"Vote on it?" I repeated incredulously. Commanders, I wanted to point out, did not wait for those under their command to vote whether or not they would follow orders! But that's exactly what the rats had done. "I see."

So passed the afternoon. I saw nothing of Retren at all, though I roamed about trying to find him.

By dinner there was an air of expectation, and it was no surprise when Nalenda rose and said there would be a celebration in the main kiln basement. Certain chores were cancelled, and everyone who had drums was to bring them.

I was not in the mood for a celebration. Of course, I never had been; I'd thought they were senseless and boring, especially the poetry stuff from south of the border. Though I did like a good, rousing ballad, such as the ancient ballad "Yvana Ride Thunder"—so ancient that no one quite knew where Yvana had even been back then— which was mostly the sort of thing that got sung and danced to, I was glad to see.

The only jolt was early on, when Tdor whispered to me, "Retren passed the word that the king doesn't want mournings for the little princess. He says we didn't know her, so he'd take the wish for the deed."

Retren said. But not to me.

The kiln basement, so warm during winter, was too warm now that spring was here; they would be letting the kiln cool for summer very soon, and laundry would be drying in the sun. When those who liked to dance ended up red-faced and sweaty, Ramond and a couple of the rats got up and did a skit, likening Imry Llyenthur to a rabbit. The younger sorts, especially the little pottery prenties and runners, found this hilarious, so of course Keth and Nollard added in a lot of fart noises and the like.

The laughter was contagious, and even Nalenda was laughing by the end. And that gave me an idea.

After another long song, which everyone seemed to know, and to join in on, then Nalenda said it was midnight, and the next day was a long one. She said everyone would be able to say goodbye "to those departing" tomorrow—if the weather permitted departures.

The screech of benches and rustle and shuffle of movement began. Glances flicked back and forth. Our Methden people stayed.

When the rest were gone, the circle drew together at the open-fireplace end of the huge room. The king sat on the floor, and the rest arranged themselves in a half-circle before him.

Some people are leaders, and some people look to leaders. The king studied our faces before speaking. "You're the beginning of the southern border's fight to regain our kingdom. I want you to keep in mind that this is only the beginning. We will only be successful when we rebuild, and make Marloven Hess better than before. That will be Norsunder's true defeat. So. We'll need a password when I send people to you. What did you decide on?"

No one had consulted me, so I'd stayed out of it, thinking their passionate debates kind of silly. Surely communication would be changing every time the enemy overheard, or discovered, something. And they would be trying.

Kethadrend piped up, "We'll ask 'em what their favorite year was, and they say '53, and we say why, and *they* say because it's Van's. How's *that*?" 4753 being when the little princess was born.

The king's face was thoughtful, but there was a hint in the way his eyes were narrowed that he was holding in laughter. But there was no sign of this in his voice as he said, "Very well." And I knew from that he was also aware that that awkward password wouldn't last long.

Kethadrend grinned proudly and sat down.

Then Rom got up and said, "Are you going to send adults?"

The king turned his attention to Rom. The laughter was gone. "Should I not? I thought the idea was to establish a safe hideout."

There was a short angry buzz, then the king said, "Rom?" in a way that shut the teens up.

Rom had never spoken at all about his horrible home life — something I'd approved of in the old days. He'd joined us tough *and* hungry — I first met him when he was caught stealing food, and brought before Da. It was his own da who had fractured his knee beyond repairing, after being booted out of the army, none of us knew why.

Rom scowled at the floor. "No, since you're asking me."

"Why not? Think they'll take over?

"Yeah. And ruin everything. Can't trust 'em."

Sindan sighed, Tdor groaned loudly, and the rats looked puzzled.

The king stared off into the fire, then said, "You'll have to decide that among yourselves. And peacefully, or you'll have ruined everything before you ever encounter an enemy."

Rom sat down, face red. There was some hasty whispering, then the king said, "Any other problems?"

Looks sidled back and forth, but no one said anything.

The king said, "There probably will be problems developing. Usually happens when something new is organized. Don't sit on 'em. Bring 'em out right away. Work them out, and you'll find operations running smoother. We're going to be off early so we'd best grab some rest now. Ramond, Marend, I'll hand the meeting off to you two."

This was my chance. I took it.

Standing up, I said, "I cannot!"

"Cannot what?" he said, looking startled.

Every pair of eyes turned my way, round in surprise.

I walked forward, aware that for once in my life, all the courtly foolery I'd had to read since I was small was actually useful for something. If not quite what the courtiers no doubt would expect.

Pressing a hand over my heart, I proclaimed, "Though I have seen the error of my ways, the trouble I have caused, I fear, renders me lowest of the low!"

Ramond's mouth fell open, and Tdor clapped a hand over hers and made a strangled sound. The rats stared.

"Marend—" the king said in exasperation.

I said, "O kick if you must this unworthy servant, lower even than lowest of the low, nay, lower even than that—" I dropped down onto the floor, trying to sound mournful, but my voice came out sounding like the bawl of a peevish cow.

"Marend!"

I smacked my forehead on the ground. "—under-lowest of the — "

My words were lost in sudden gusts of laughter.

"All right. Cast her forth into the pits!" The king jerked his thumb over his shoulder with one hand.

They all surrounded me, pretending to yell and be fierce, and I made no effort to defend myself as they took hold of my legs and arms and tossed me into the air. I did shut my eyes, braced to crash on the ground, so certain was I of secret resentment. But they caught me, and after a couple more throws, and a lot of noise, they set me down, all laughing. I trembled all over, my emotions swooping, dizzy as a drunken bird. If birds do get drunk.

To my surprise it seemed to work. The atmosphere with the rats eased. Probably making a fool of myself did not make me any more trustworthy but it certainly made me more bearable. I saw it work, and I resolved to think more about this later.

The best was, as the meeting quickly broke up, Retren came over, and grinned at me with all his old laughter. Tdor and Ramond also approached, and Ramond started making jokes about lowness and beneath-under-down, so there was no sense of being alone, but I could tell I had done something right in his eyes as well.

As we all walked upstairs, I contrived to get Ramond and Tdor and Sindan talking about skits, and I slowed my pace — and Retren stayed with me. I said to him, "You know where you're going?"

"To all the cities, then to the capital."

No one was around. I said awkwardly, "Well — take care of yourself."

"I will, but he said — if I get sick — then we'll wait until I get better!" Ret's tone was firm, pleased, but this statement washed over me like sudden hailstones. He had misunderstood what I meant.

I couldn't let it go like that.

"I mean, come back safe. And," I added quickly, my words sounding inane in my own ears, "I'm *glad* you'll rest if you get sick. I'm sorry about all that."

"Ah." He jerked his skinny shoulders up. "I know that's how you and Da felt!"

There seemed to be nothing more to say. What was the use of telling him that the happier he was to be going, the sharper my sense of loss? Part of my sadness was at his lack of it. He was *happy to be getting away from me.* And all the grief roared back, harder than ever.

The others rejoined us, but I couldn't resent it. It was with a sense of defeat I slid out of the group, and went down to my room. I had no desire to say goodbye.

But just before dawn came a tap at my door.

"Marend," the king said, "get dressed and come with us? We've something for you before we go."

I couldn't see their faces. It was yet too dark, and his whisper told me nothing.

"Coming," I said.

They went out. I jerked my clothes on and jammed my feet into my boots without bothering with socks.

I caught up with them at the stairs to the roof. The air was cold and damp but the rain had swept southward.

On the roof we walked to the worn railing on the east side of the building.

Retren was silent. The king said, "Marend, your brother wants you to have this gift. A treasure of the lighters—but it can be a two-edged sword." His tone was quiet and almost *guarded*-seeming, but there was nothing in his stance to indicate anger or combat-tension. The light was still too faint to create any but confused shadows on his face. From long habit I stiffened, thinking as I always had that pain can be conquered, and a commander is better for having been through the fire of various tests—

"Face the east," the king said, a tremor of humor in his voice.

Surprised, I did so, and waited. This was something I had done many times: the morning Ramond and I first broached the subject of truce floated to my mind like a leaf from the bottom of a stream, then disappeared again. I looked to the forest-edged mountains, where the sun rimmed the uneven line.

Suddenly the king's voice was in my mind. There was that peculiar sense of expansion but no pain as he said, "See it now through Retren's eyes."

My gaze lifted eastward again, as the sun crowned the

mountains with pale fire, golden light shafting across the valley floor to warm the edges of trees and buildings. There the light limned a plow horse as it pranced in the crisp air, its breath a soft cloud, and beyond the horse a woman with a basket walked toward the far-lying vegetable garden. The light illumined her cotton shirt and old gown, and her ruddy face.

I wanted to dance in the silence, to give form to the nameless feeling taking wing inside me, up and up toward the rising sun, higher, toward the fleeing stars. How to describe this giddy sense of internal expanse? The nearest word is power, but a kind utterly without the urge to rule, to subjugate, or to destroy. I wanted to scream, to laugh, to run my brains out. I knew if I stretched my arms out I could touch the sun—

Then around the edges the vision began to glitter and tingle, then start to fade—

"*Breathe*, Marend!" the king uttered a quick, soft laugh.

I turned my eyes away, breathing deeply. There was Retren's light-warmed face, expectant, smiling. A few feet away the king glanced away and out, as if he were seeing straight beyond the sun.

"Did you *see* it? Do you understand?" Retren asked.

It was beauty, so simple a word. But I had never understood its allure. Its intensity.

"He said *he* only understood it *recently!*" he went on wonderingly, then with a little satisfaction: "I want the words to describe that feeling. I am going to find them, even if I have to learn a lot of other languages. I *want* to!"

The king stirred. "Time we were off. Farm's up soon."

"Our horses are waiting." Retren pointed down at the stable. "We wanted to see you first."

I gazed in surprise, not comprehending how the king could throw this gift into my hands, then turn away. But he hadn't, not really. It was Retren's gift. And *he* was going away.

Cold fingers briefly touched my hand. "Bye, Marend," Retren said almost inaudibly, ducked his head, and walked to the stairs, and vanished.

The king turned to follow. I said, my voice choked, but I didn't even care, "You said understanding and forgiveness don't follow each other. What you didn't say is that

trust doesn't either. And it's the hardest of all to get back."
When he didn't deny it, I burst out, "Which leaves me with
what? With nothing." I gritted my teeth against a sob, but
it pressed mercilessly against my ribs.

"What you are left with," the king said, "is a future.
The both of you. Make it a good one, Marend."

He lifted a hand and followed Retren, adding over his
shoulder, "Tell the potters we had to get an early start."

They both had vanished, then reappeared smaller
down below. Neither looked back as they got on their
horses, and then rode away, to be lost almost immediately
among the trees growing alongside the stream.

I turned my head, my throat aching, my eyes stinging.
They had given me a gift, and then left me bereft.

After a time, as I struggled against tears, they
reappeared on a hillock on the other side of the stream, tiny
figures both. The light was day-strong as they turned and
waved, then cantered northward.

I watched them until they were out of sight.

It has taken longer to write all this down than I had thought
it would, and there were times (particularly when I was
tired, and I had to write the parts I hate) when I was ready
to give up.

But I wrote down a little each night all this summer,
after digging. Then, after the vagabond came and finished
our two underground hideouts for us, after our drills. We
are very good at woodland stealth now. Even I have
adopted mocs. We can get from one end of the forest to the
other without disturbing a leaf, and the king was right —
there is an odd, but definite, sense of awareness between
the forest-life and ourselves.

Only one person has arrived so far, besides the vagabond, a young cavalry officer. He fit in with us with little
stir.

There has been no word or sight of Retren or the king.
Which is as well. I had wanted to finish this record before
I see them again, and do what I feel I have to. Since I
finished writing this yesterday, tonight I'll tell Tdor I'm
leaving.

I intend to return to Darchelde, as I promised, but first I am going to use all those stealth skills I've learned, and bring this to Methden, to give to you, Mother.

I know trust is too much to expect. Forgiveness might be as well, but what I'm hoping for is for us to find some understanding.

Author's Note

Marend's record runs alongside the first two books in *The Norsunder War*, *Ship Without Sails*, and *Seek to Hold the Wind*.

About the Author

Sherwood Smith writes fantasy, science fiction, and historical fiction. Her full bibliography can be found on her website at https://www.sherwoodsmith.net

About Book View Cafe

Book View Café is an author-owned cooperative of professional writers, publishing in a variety of genres including fantasy, science fiction, romance, mystery, and more.

Its authors include New York Times and USA Today best-sellers as well as winners and nominees of many prestigious awards such as the Agatha Award, Hugo Award, Lambda Literary Award, Locus Award, Nebula Award, RITA Award, Philip K. Dick Award, World Fantasy Award, and many others.

Since its debut in 2008, Book View Café has gained a reputation for producing high quality books in both print and electronic form. BVC's e-books are DRM-free and distributed around the world.

Book View Café's monthly newsletter includes new releases, specials, author news, and event announcements. To sign up, visit:
 https://www.bookviewcafe.com/bookstore/newsletter/

Made in the USA
Middletown, DE
04 October 2022

11745908R00096